Otis Flagg
and the
Promise of Time

#2 in the trilogy.

The Saga Continues

For my very good friend —
Gene !
Enjoy
Brian Pb

BRIAN PETERSON

This is a work of fiction. All characters and events in this book are fictional. All persons in this book resembling anyone or anybody living or dead is purely a coincidence.

This book is for the dreamer in all of us.

Thanks to Zak who finished what he started and to Judy, whose patience, support, and input helped me to complete this work.

Time to Ponder

Time is the true measure of all things.
Time is the great healer.
Time can be remembered or forgotten .
Time can be used or abused.
Time is limited yet has no limits.
Time can be good or bad depending how it is
used.
Time is more precious than diamonds, silver,
or gold.
Time is priceless yet if squandered, it is
worthless.
The time you keep is not really yours, even
when it appears to be all you have.
Time is endless and what goes around comes
around.
Lastly and most importantly….. the time you
waste having fun, is not necessarily wasted
time!

Have fun,
Brian Peterson
April 2018

Other Works by Brian Peterson

FOWL PLAY

A Three Act Comedy for ages 8 to 80.

DIE HAPPY

A Three Act Fun Thriller
and soon to be novel.

THREE SHORT PLAYS
Volumes One and Two

DON'T JUST WAIT TABLES, DAZZLE THEM
A self help manual on customer service for
restaurant waitstaff.

Available online.

Prologue

If you are about to read this narrative and haven't already done so, I would suggest reading *The Life and Times of Otis Flagg* to get a better understanding of who Otis Flagg is. This is not mandatory of course and you should still be able to enjoy what you are about to read. Although this was not written as a series, the story in these pages begins where the first book ended.

Otis Flagg's story is about a man in his golden years who now spends time watching the world go by outside his window. Upon receiving and discovering the powers of a strange blue bottle, he totally changed his life in ways he never could have imagined. He had lived through good and bad times, wasted time and found ways to save time, but he had never been able to transcend time…….. until now!

So then, Otis Flagg's story is a story of time. It is a story of how he learned to travel through time and transcend his once perceived boundaries. His gateway into these various worlds is within the blue bottle. A bottle containing a time portal that allows him to visit different time periods and places and then a way back to the present.

In this book, Otis's saga continues. After traveling back in time he is reunited with the love of his life, Sara, only to realize even though they are together, they are in separate time planes as two different species. Their shared hope of reuniting in the same time, as humans, rests on Otis's success traveling back through the time portal to find the time keeper known as The Source.

While Sara, as a feline, must remain in the present dealing with neighbors of Otis, he enters the time portal and finds himself in the year 1846 and the wild west. Here he must dodge bullets and the hangman's noose if he is to find The Source of all Time. He also must stay ahead of hombres who are much more used to living in the violent times of the old west.

Life becomes very challenging for Otis and Sara and they must keep their wits about them to survive. Who is Otis Flagg? The answer may be in the pages ahead....

Enjoy this second helping of Otis Flagg!

Brian Peterson

The Saga Continues...

Sara

Otis arrived home just after 8 o'clock as the sun was setting on a warm summer evening. The neighborhood was quiet and his next door neighbor's house was dark. He was hoping he could get in his house without Margie and Bill coming over to check in on him. He especially didn't want to explain to them bringing home a new cat.

He pulled into his driveway, killed the car engine, and waited a minute to make sure he hadn't been seen or heard. When no lights came on in the neighbor's house, he got out of the car and carried Sara into her new home.

He put her down just inside the door and before he could say anything she scampered off into the darkness of the house.

"Sara..Sara!" he called out, closing the door.

"Kitty kitty kitty," he called a second time as he switched on the hall light.

Out of nowhere the cat came bounding around a hall table and jumped up into his arms. She made a meowing noise followed by soft purring and then, "Otis, you found me!"

Otis was stunned. "Sara, did you just talk?! How can that be?" Otis's eyes were blinking. Sara squirmed in his arms until she could face him. Her eyes were fixed on his.

"No, I can't talk like you, but you and only you, can understand me. It has something to do with our prior connection, which has split into two parallel time planes. Maybe a glitch of some sorts."

Otis was speechless. He looked down at her in his arms, all soft and cuddly. "How,....what happened to you? How long have you been this way?" Otis was full of questions even though he understood how easy it was to change species. He had done so in a parallel life. He had crossed over and discovered himself as a pig. Thinking about that day made him shudder even now. Hopefully Sara could tell him how she became trapped in her present condition. Maybe there was a way to reverse it.

Sara snuggled closer. "Why don't you sit down, you must be tired after driving all day?"

Otis had spent the day driving from a rest area somewhere in Iowa, a half way point in returning from Colorado.

Otis smiled and studied her face. Do cats worry? He could see Sara had a look of worry in her face.

"Yes, yes, I'd like to sit, we'll go to study, its just down the hall."

Otis carried her down the hall and into his study where he placed her on the desk. It was dark in the room and as Otis switched on the desk lamp, Sara surveyed the desk top, creeping from side to side and front to rear. Otis chuckled. "Does it pass your inspection, kitty cat?"

She flicked her tail as she sat back on her haunches and looked up at him.

"Please don't call me kitty cat and as for me being inquisitive, you can never be too careful Otis Flagg. I could have been compromised on more than one occasion not being aware of my surroundings."

Otis understood and sat down at his desk.

"Forgive me, I understand what…."

She interrupted him, "No apologies needed. I've had to learn to always beware and look around every corner. Cats are curious or didn't you know that?" Sara was purring again and Otis thought he detected a smile also.

"Sara, How did you ever learn to transcend time and end up being a feline? Obviously you became trapped."

Sara's tail waved slowly and evenly behind her as she relived her story in her mind.

"It all seems so long ago." she began. "I wasn't sure what happened to you that night in Colorado and was totally devastated when you disappeared."

Otis's own memory returned to that night.

"Sara I am so sorry," he began, but she didn't let him finish.

"It's okay Otis. I understand everything."
Otis gently touched her head. "I don't know
how you could."
"Do you remember Linda?" Sara asked.

"Sure! Your friend and our rafting guide!"
Otis answered as he visualized her in his
mind's eye.
Sara continued,
"Yes, we were great friends, but drifted apart
in the years after you disappeared." Sara got
up on all fours and began walking around the
desk top as she talked.
"I hadn't seen her in years and then one day
out of the blue, she showed up at my door.
She had been drinking and I could tell she had
been crying. I opened the door and let her in."
Sara paused and flicked her tail. Otis
understood her anguish.
"Go on, I'm listening." he said in a soft voice.
"Like I said, I hadn't seen her in ages and
unbeknownst to me she was still with the
owner of that rafting place. Toby, remember
him?"
"Yes, Toby the rafting outfitter. I remember
him well. He and I shared a secret about time
travel. The day I met him he told me about
someone back here, in this very house that
might be trapped. Trapped like you are now.
That's why I left that night and couldn't tell
you why."

Sara came and sat directly in front of Otis. "I understand that now." Then she froze and crouched. Her ears arched back as she took a defensive position. Slowly looking from side to side she whispered, "Did you hear that?!"

Otis cocked his head and whispered back. "I don't hear a thing,"

"You have mice." Sara replied. "And they are busy."

Otis was in no mood to hear about mice right now. "I'll set a trap later, please go on and tell me about Toby."

Sara's eyes searched the dark corner of the room before returning to focus on Otis. "No need for a trap, Otis." She smiled and continued with her story.

"Linda and Toby lived together and one night after he hadn't come home, she accused him of seeing someone else. Since it had happened on more than one occasion, Linda told him she'd had enough and walked out.

To get her back, Toby confessed to her his ability to transcend time and to prove it to her took her to a cave not far from the rafting office."

Otis interrupted her, "I think I know what was in that cave."

"Yes, a hot spring containing a time portal. It was there he was able to prove to her his absences. She also learned the truth about the conversation you two had had. When we couldn't find you that night, he had known what had happened but didn't say anything." She flipped her tail, "I was so pissed when she told me this."

"My poor Sara. Please go on."

"This news was not only shocking to me, it was preposterous! Her showing up out of the blue telling me stories of time portals and time travel had me thinking she was in a drunken stupor. I was about to show her the door when he knocked."

"He?" asked Otis.

"Toby, himself. I opened the door and there he stood all sullen looking. He nodded his head and asked if he could come in. I opened the door and he joined Linda and me at my kitchen table. He began talking and collaborated Linda's story. To remove any doubt he said he would take me to the cave so I could see for myself."

Otis shifted in his desk chair. "I see where this is heading."

Sara was up on all fours once again, walking around. "The following weekend I arranged to meet them at the rafting office. I drove over to Glenwood wondering if I'd lost my mind for doing such a thing.

Shortly after I arrived we left the office and walked up a trail along the river that led us between some huge boulders. Ten minutes later we came upon a stand of bushes that covered a cave opening. If you didn't know it was there, you wouldn't have seen it. Anyway once inside you could hear a gurgling hot spring not too far from the entrance. The cave was full of steam that was escaping up through a shaft above the pool of hot water. Coming down through the shaft was a strange beam of light, illuminating the pool. It was an eerily beautiful sight."

Otis's eyes widened as he looked at Sara. Her eyes were staring off into space as she relived this moment for him. She then continued.

"Toby then told us he would go into the portal and return with proof of his movement into the future and back. I watched him walk into the pool beneath the beam and something flashed and he was gone!"

Sara looked up at Otis. Her tail was now whipping back and forth like that of an agitated feline. Otis said nothing, fearing it would be similar to waking someone having a dream.

"A few seconds passed and there was a second flash of light. Magically, there he was and in his hand was a photograph of the three of us returning to the rafting office. This was the picture one of his employees would take of us twenty minutes from now. I was still somewhat skeptical, but since he had actually disappeared before my eyes, then reappeared, I believed his story. I apologized for doubting him and that prompted him to suggest that I use the portal to find you, Otis."

Otis got a look of despair in his face. "Oh my God."

"Otis, it wasn't easy, I was tormented just by the thought. You know I have a son, your son, and I didn't know what to do. I didn't want to abandon him, but at the same time I had to see if I could find you. After Toby explained to me it would be safe to use the portal if I came back within 72 hours, I decided to do it."

"And did you tell young Otis what you were doing?" Otis asked. He knew of their son, but because of the conflicts in time, he couldn't introduce himself to him just yet. The time would have to be just right.

Sara sighed. "No. I couldn't tell him what I was up to. Linda said he could stay with her, so the following day I took off from work and told my boss and neighbors that I was going hiking along the river over in Glenwood Springs. I met Toby and Linda that afternoon and they took me back up to the cave.

Once back inside the cave the hot spring still bubbled and swirled. The steaming water and the beam of light were mesmerizing and when I stepped into it, I felt whisked away.

I don't know what happened to me but when I went through the portal…….."

A look of confusion filled Sara's face and Otis put a hand on her head to comfort her.
"It's alright Sara. When you came through to this side you were a feline. Why though didn't you just turn around and go back?"

"I didn't understand what had happened and I panicked. I ran as fast as I could out of that cave and hid under some bushes until the authorities caught and imprisoned me. I couldn't go back."

"Authorities?" Otis asked with a quizzed look.
"The humans. We cats call all humans authorities, the keepers. In this case it was a man named Christopher Borders. He was camping with his family and caught me while out relieving himself. He made me a gift for his young daughter, Sissy.
Otis's mouth was open as he gasped. "And you couldn't get back to the portal within the 72 hours!"

"No. I was a prisoner of the Borders. No one ever found my body and presumed I'd drowned. My poor son Otis became an orphan."
Otis and Sara sat quietly for a minute.
"How long were you with this family?"
"At least five human years." Sara answered.
"They lived in Glenwood Springs and I finally

managed to escape to make my way back to Rifle, but that was no easy task."

Otis reached over and picked Sara up and placed her in his lap. "My poor kitten, you are safe now and I am sure we can figure out how to get you back into this human plane again!"

"You old dreamer you." Sara said looking up into Otis's face.

"No, not a dream. Did Toby say anything about a Source to you?"

"A source? No, what kind of source?"

"You know, a god or higher being. The man that introduced me to time travel spoke of the Source. A spiritual being that controlled all movement in time."

Sara jumped from Otis's lap back to the desk top.

"And you believed him?"

"I didn't believe anything he said until I experienced moving about in time. He didn't lie to me about that."

"Where is this Source and how do we find it?" Sara was becoming curious once again.

As they talked there was a knock on the front door. Sara jumped to the floor, her tail raised in the air.

Otis raised his hand. "Just stay in here, I'll see who it is. I've got a good idea it's my neighbor. Don't worry, you are safe here."

Otis left her in the study and made his way to

the front door. Switching on the outdoor light,
he saw his visitor was indeed his neighbor,
Margie Case.

He unlocked the door and opened it.

"Hello Margie." he said trying to sound
friendly.

"Otis Flagg, I've been worried sick about you.
I haven't seen you in two days and was afraid
you were ill or something. Then I saw this
strange car in your drive and thought I'd better
see if you were okay."

"Oh, you know me I'm fine. I rented a car and
went down to Iowa to visit an old friend. The
rental company will pick up the car
tomorrow." Otis was becoming more fluid
with his lies.

"Well aren't you going to invite me in?" his
neighbor boldly asked. "I can't stay long, but
I'd like to make sure you've got enough of the
proper food on hand."

Margie had taken it upon herself to watch over
Otis as he got older and although Otis didn't
mind being fussed over, he didn't have time
for it tonight.

"Margie thanks, but I've been driving all day
and I'm tired. Fact is I was just about ready for
bed. I assure you I have a pantry full of good
food, most of it stuff you brought over last
week."

Margie gave him the eye as she tilted her head.
"Well okay then. We can talk more tomorrow.

I have to worry you know." She gave him a big smile, turned and walked back to her house next door.

Otis breathed a sigh of relief and switched the light off. Coming back into the study, Sara was back on the desk again waiting for him.

"It was my neighbor, just as I thought. She's gone now," he said somewhat relieved.

Sara had become impatient. "Okay Otis, how do we find this Source?"

Otis bit his lip as he lapsed into thought. "I'm not sure. I do know that I'm pretty tired right now. I've been driving all day Sara and I'd like to sleep on it. If there is a Source, we'll find him, I promise you that."

Night Moves

Otis and Sara talked for another few minutes or so, mostly about the house. Otis had stopped on the way home and bought a bag of kitty litter. As Sara followed him from room to room, she watched him as he fixed a cat box for her and set down a bowl of fresh water. Once he had her taken care of her needs for the evening he gave Sara a kiss on the head and said good night.

Sara followed Otis into his bedroom and jumped up on the bed as he pulled the covers up to his chin.

"I hope you won't mind if I curl up here on your bed,"she said snuggling up close to his side.

Otis looked over and smiled, "I hope you never sleep anywhere else."

He reached over to his bedside table and switched the light off. The room went dark and Otis was soon asleep.

As for Sara, her eyesight allowed her to see very well in the absence of light in the room. She couldn't see rich colors or fine details, but being a feline she had perfect night vision. She lay on the bed listening to Otis's breathing become slower and slower as he drifted deeper into sleep. Being nocturnal, she soon got up and jumped to the floor. She had wanted to explore the house and all its nooks and crannies and now was the time.

The bedroom door had been left open a crack and she slipped out into the hallway, her tail up behind her slowly waving from side to side. Not making a sound, she crept down the hallway and came into the living room. The room was not that large with only a few pieces of furniture taking up space. There was one recliner by the only window in the room, a stuffed sofa against one wall, and a matching stuffed chair. A small lamp table separated the sofa and chair.

Sara stayed close to the wall and followed it around to the sofa where she found that she fit nicely behind it. It would be a good place to hide if need be, she thought.

She moved along the wall and came out at the other end of the sofa where Otis's recliner sat. She jumped up into it and from there to the windowsill.

The curtain had been pulled back and she viewed the outdoors through the window. The house next door was close, but not as close as the house, where she had lived before. Just then a light came on in the neighboring house. Sara crouched down and focused her eyes on the window. She saw movement, an authoritarian figure opened the refrigerator, closed it and left the room. The room then went dark again and Sara jumped off the windowsill to continue her tour.

She left the living room and crept back to the bedroom where Otis was now snoring. She loved this human. He was not like all the other so called authorities. She would find her human self again and they would be together forever.

She moved back into the hallway and crept past the entry to the study. She had pretty much explored that room and she wanted to check out the kitchen where she had heard the mice earlier.

As she neared the kitchen her instincts caused her to became even more stealth like. She let her eyes do the work, surveying every inch of the floor. She saw nothing and nothing moved. She slowly entered the room and moving through the darkness to the small kitchen table, she leapt up onto the table in one jump.

All remained quiet. Sara slowly moved across the table top, moving closer to her objective, the cooking range. From this tactical point she could peer down to the area running behind the stove.

She crouched and waited, all the while keeping her sharp eyes on the first thing to move. Behind her, her tail slowly glided back and forth.

She didn't have to wait very long. She heard it before it came into view. From along the wall behind the stove, a large gray female mouse came creeping out and stopped, its round black nose twitching in the air.

Mice have very poor eyesight in the darkness and Sara knew this, but she also knew they could move very fast in panic situations, some up to 12 feet a second. Sara doubted this one could move that fast, she was too fat from taking advantage of Otis's hospitality.

Sara was as still as a tomb. Only her tail moved about in the darkness until she saw the mouse inch out farther from behind the stove. Sara waited until the mouse wrongly determined it was alone in the room and ventured out from behind the stove . Without a sound Sara flung herself through the air and down upon the unsuspecting rodent, sinking her teeth into the terrified mouse's head. It was only able to make one tiny squeak before Sara's jaws crushed the mouse's skull.

Sara felt jubilant with her kill and couldn't wait to show Otis her trophy. She hadn't been here twenty four hours and was already earning her keep!

She held the mouse tightly in her mouth. It was a female and that meant there were other mice here, probably a whole family. She would get them all! With that thought she trotted with her trophy back to Otis's bed. She wanted him to see it first thing when he awoke. She jumped up on the bed and dropped the mouse on the pillow next to his snoring head. She had now earned herself some rest, curled up on the bed and closed her eyes.

Morning came early for Otis. He was awake at 5:30 just as light from outside begun to filter in though the window blinds. His eyes open, he lay there feeling the stiffness in his joints until the urge to urinate overcame the stiffness and he threw the blanket back to get out of bed. Doing this, he caught the dead mouse's body and flung it against the wall. It made a loud thump as it hit and scared Otis to the point he almost lost wet himself.

"Son of a bitch, what was that!? he yelled. Sara who had gotten up an hour earlier, came trotting into the room, tail on high.

"What is it? Are you okay?" she jumped up into the bed.

"There was something in the bed!" It was still dark enough in the room that he couldn't see the dead rodent on the floor.

"Otis, Otis, its alright." Sara said trying her best to settle him down. "It's only a mouse I killed in the night. It can't hurt you."

Otis was now standing at the foot of the bed. "What the hell was it doing in my bed?"

"I killed it for you! It has been stealing from you and now it is dead! I thought you'd be happy, I'm earning my keep."

Sara jumped off the bed and grabbing the dead mouse with her jaws, ran with it to the kitchen.

Otis was now fully awake and followed her knowing that he may have over reacted.

"Sara, I'm sorry. I didn't mean to scold you for bringing that thing to my bed. I wasn't fully awake and it scared the hell out of me."

Sara was waiting in the kitchen and had had a chance to rationalize her actions.

"You're right. I shouldn't have brought it's body to your bed. I had forgotten how much most authorities feared rodents"

Otis came up to where Sara had taken up a place by the back door. "Please don't think of

me as the authorities? I'm very happy that you rid this house of that thing."
Sara flicked her tail. "I'm sorry Otis. I don't think of you as the authorities and any further mice I catch will just go outside just like this one, if you'll open the door for me."

Otis opened the door and Sara grabbed the mouse and took it outdoors to a place near the alley where she knew neighborhood feral cats would find and devour it. Otis waited by the door to let her in when she returned.
The rest of the morning was for breakfast and making plans to find a way to return Sara to her human form. Otis decided he would go through the time portal again and search for the Source that Twirly had told him about. There must be a way to find him Otis told Sara. Sara was more fearful of the plan.
"Otis, I'm afraid. You can never be sure what happens when you go through a portal. I'm proof of that. I don't want to lose you again. I'd rather you stay here with me. There must be another way."
They were back in the study now and she was sitting on the desk.
Otis was sitting in his desk chair and was patting her head. "Sara, we both know there is no other way. You will be fine here while I'm gone. There is plenty of food and litter for you until I get back and that will be within three

days."

They sat in silence for the next few minutes and Sara finally nodded her approval even though her tail was snapping about with nervous twitches.

Otis opened the desk drawer and took out the blue bottle.

"I love you Sara." he told her as he worked the cork free. There was a rush of air and light and he was gone. Sara felt a chill run from her neck to the tip of her tail. Now she could only wait.

Jack Rand

Otis opened his eyes and found himself seated and bouncing around in a stagecoach. Sitting beside him was a large burly man with a pitted face and a thick mustache. Otis had no idea where he was and outside the stagecoach window told him little. There moving slowly past his window he saw a barren landscape cluttered with brush and cactus. He could also hear the pounding hooves of the horses pulling the coach he was in.

He went to move his hand and found it was tied to his other one with a rawhide strip.

"Hey what the hell is this?!" he demanded out loud.

The burly man next to him had been dozing and upon hearing Otis's demand, opened his eyes. He had a Colt .45 revolver in his hand

and pointed the end of the barrel at Otis's head.

"Take it easy Rand, don't even think about getting away. Your arse belongs to me!" His upper lip had curled up in a smile, showing his yellow stained and crooked teeth.

Otis was confused. "Rand? I'm afraid you got the wrong man. My name is Otis, Otis Flagg!"

"Sure you are, then who's this?" Burly asked with a broad grin, taking a folded wanted poster out of his vest pocket and showing it to Otis.

Otis looked the poster and saw a likeness of his face below large block letters that read:

WANTED
JACK RAND
$1000 REWARD

He was shocked, "That's not me! I don't know who this is or where you got it, but my name is Otis! Otis Flagg from..." He stopped in mid sentence. His memory had lapsed.

The burly man put his thick tongue between his teeth and gave Otis an elbow to the side of his head, knocking him unconscious.

"I got you Rand!" the burly man shouted loudly in a victorious manner. "You won't get away this time!" He found this funny and laughed making him wet himself. He then screamed, "God damn, now look what you made me do!" He savagely gave Otis another sharp elbow to the side of his head.

Two miles later the stagecoach reached one of the many stagecoach stations along the trail connecting Butte Ridge and Devils Heart, Texas. The driver hollered above the noise down to his coach passengers to alert them of the impending stop.

Burly looked out his window and scanned the area for an ambush. He feared Rand's gang would be looking to spring him free and he was not about to let that happen.

Not seeing any signs of anything out of the ordinary, he grabbed Otis by his light jacket and shook him. "Wake up Rand, I got to take a dump and I ain't letting you out of my sight!"

The stagecoach relay station was in the middle of nowhere, just off the trail and was made up of a small shabby one-story house that sat next to a horse corral and barn.

The stagecoach driver drove the horses into the station yard and was met by the station man. He was an experienced cowhand hired by the stage line, adept at caring for horses, the company's main asset.

As the horses came to a stop in front of the corral, the station man came running out and took hold of the lead horse's bridle and calmed the horses while the coach driver jumped down from his seat to assist.

Otis was regaining consciousnesses, but his head throbbed where Burly had caught him with his elbow. His right cheek was also puffy, causing him to squint so he could see. He wracked his memory trying to understand what was happening to him as the stagecoach stopped.

He heard the driver climbing down off the rig and then opening the door.

"We'll be here about 30 minutes gents. The station man's woman usually has some grub ready inside." The driver was pointing at the ramshackle house with his thumb over his shoulder.

"Where's the outhouse?" Burly hoarsely barked.

"Round back that way," the station man said pointing to the corner of the house. "I need a new one dug so it stinks bad back round there."

Burly grabbed Otis by the shoulder and almost pushed him out through the door. "Come on Rand, you're goin' with me."

Otis caught himself from falling to the ground as Burly jumped out of the coach behind him. When Burly landed on his feet and stood up, Otis saw why he had been intimidated by this man. He was all of 6'5" tall and broad as a horse through the shoulders. His most intimidating feature though was his Colt .45 single action revolver, which he kept in his hand. Otis had been able to count eight notches in the wooden handle, but was unsure of what they meant. He had a good idea, but didn't care to find out.

Burly, standing up, prodded Otis toward the back of the house as the station man's wife watched nervously from the window.

"Come on, move it!" he grunted to Otis. "You already made me piss myself and if I shit myself I'll be wiping my arse with you!"

As the burly man and Otis came out of the coach, a pair of eyes in the horse barn, was peering through a crack in the sun weathered siding.

"It's Rand!" whispered the voice with the eyes.

"And the bounty hunter got him?" a second voice asked.

"Yeah, it's that snake Bryan Bodie. He's a big son of a bitch ain't he?!" came the first voice again.

"What they doin'?"

"They just went around the back, probably to find the outhouse."

The two men watching from the horse barn were part of Jack Rand's outfit. One of them was Evert Dodge, a gunslinger from Deadwood South Dakota who was Rand's right hand man. The second man was Randolph Coats, the one Rand called on to collect his debts for him. Both men were masters at escape and wanted in different territories.

The station man and the stagecoach driver had unhitched the team of horses and ran them into the corral where there was hay and fresh water. When they came into the barn to fetch the fresh team of horses, Dodge and Coats were waiting for them.

The driver was the first to see them. "Hey, what the hell!?"

"Quiet! Dodge said in a loud whisper. "Or I'll blow that flappin' tongue clean out of your mouth!" He held a long barreled revolver up to the driver's cheek. Coats stood beside him pointing his Winchester rifle at the two.

"Drop you guns on the floor and get over by the fence." He pointed to the wooden partition in the barn that separated horse compartments.

The two men did as they were told and allowed Coats to tie their wrists behind them and to the fence. After gagging them each he said. "Now you two gentlemen stay here and keep quiet for the next fifteen minutes and no one gets hurt. Mama will be out and cut you free after we leave, you got that?"

Both men shook their heads yes. They had seen their faces on wanted posters and knew they were dangerous.

Dodge and Coats left them in the barn and

quietly ran around to the back of the house where the outhouse was located.

Rounding the corner of the house they saw Otis with his head down and on his knees in front of the open outhouse door.

"Jesus Christ, look at the boss's face!" Dodge whispered. "Bodie must of blind sided him. The right side of his face looks like horse meat!"

"I can see the boss, but can you see that fucking bounty hunter?!" Coats muttered in a very low voice as he gritted his teeth.

"He's got to be sitting inside. I say we surprise the shit right out of him!." Dodge was building up a rage.

Coats held out his rifle. "Annabelle here is gonna help us!"

The two men left where they'd been kneeling by the house and circled around and up behind the outhouse. As they moved in behind the dilapidated shed one took each side. Otis looked up to see Dodge, who instantly put his finger to his lips in a shushing signal.

Big Bodie sat inside on the wooden boards with a hole cut in them with his trousers down around his ankles. Each time he strained, pushed, and grunted he would look at Otis kneeling before him and make a snide remark. "That one was for your mama!" he'd say with a loud cackle. "And that one was for your sister!"

It was after that remark that Coats stepped around the front side of the outhouse and yelled, "And this one's for you!" before crashing the butt of his rifle into Bodie's forehead.

His head snapped backward and his forehead split open spraying blood out and over his bare knees and legs. His hand groped wildly for his pistol which he had placed beside him on the seat, but blood from the large gash above his eyes kept him from seeing anything.

"Don't move you big dumb bastard or I'll give your nose a third hole!" Screamed Dodge who had come around the other side of the tiny building.

Bodie realized he was at a very big disadvantage and stopped any movement. While Coats kept his rifle on Bodie, Dodge helped Otis to his feet and untied his hands.

"Are you okay, Boss?" he asked an unsteady Otis.

Otis had no idea who any of these men were, but knew the two that had just freed him must be the good guys.

"I think so." he replied meekly.

"What should we do with this cocksucker?" Dodge was pointing at the bloodied hulk Otis had called Burly. Otis didn't know what to say and shook his head.

"Don't worry about it then. We'll take care of

it. We got your horse and saddlebags in the barn with ours. Head for the barn and we'll catch up."

Otis was still confused but made his way around the house and toward the barn while Dodge and Coats took care of Bodie.

Using the rawhide strap that Bodie had used on Otis, they tied his hands behind his back and used his belt to strap his feet together. As he lie on the ground in front of the outhouse he begged them to leave him alone. The two men ignored him and pushed the tiny wooden framed building off the hole that had been dug for the station's waste.

The stench was overwhelming causing both men to fight off gagging..

In the bottom third of the six foot deep hole, flies buzzed around soft clumps and pillars of decaying human feces.

Holding their breathing they pushed Bodie over the edge and he landed head first in the soupy slop. He squirmed and wiggled to do all that he could to keep from drowning. In doing so he managed to keep his head above the surface and continue to breath. Even tied up the way he was, he managed to right himself so he was sitting upright. He shook his head back and forth like a wild animal to overcome the sting in his eyes from the liquid ammonia. "I'll find you, you bloody bastards!" he screamed, his voice echoing inside the dark hole. "I'll fucking find you and you'll be mine!"

Dodge and Coats with Otis in tow, rode out of the stagecoach station on horseback and headed South across the brush covered land Otis had seen from his ride in the stagecoach. Otis was still clueless to who his companions were, but at least he had gotten away from the Burly guy. As he rode, he wondered what they had done with him. He wondered if they had killed him.

Sara

After Otis disappeared Sara spent the first ten minutes pacing about as she worried about his departure into the unknown.
In the second hour of his absence her memory of him began to fade as her feline psyche began to reclaim itself.
She jumped off the desk and left the study. Looking first toward the kitchen, she trotted down the hallway and into the living room where the sun was shining in through a window. At first she sat on the floor where the rays of the warm sunshine were fixed. It was the perfect place to give herself a bath. As she sat there first licking her paw and then using it to wash behind her one ear before switching paws, she realized if she jumped up and sat on

the windowsill, she could take full advantage
of the sun and its comforting heat.

The warmth felt heavenly and she began to
purr ever so softly and soon she was consumed
with thoughts of taking a nap. The window
sill was just wide enough for her to lie down.
She did so and closed her eyes.

Next door Otis's neighbor Margie Case, was
busy at her kitchen sink. Looking out through
the sink window, she saw Sara lying in Otis's
window.

Surprised to see a cat, she called out to her
husband Bill..

"Bill, come quickly and look! Otis has a cat!"
Bill came into the kitchen and joined Margie by
the window..

"While I'll be damned." he said. "You were
over there last evening, didn't he say anything
about having a cat?"

"No. But he was acting kind of strange, now
that I think about it. He said he'd been driving
all day and was too tired to let me in. You
know Bill, I think Otis is getting too old to be
out driving, especially all day long."

Bill looked at Otis's empty driveway. "What
was he driving?"

"He had a rental car, from some company that
picks it up at your door I guess. At least that's
what he said. It's gone now so they must have
come and got it."

Across the driveway, in Otis's house, Sara heard a noise in another room and left her perch on the window sill.

Bill noticed the empty window first.. "Hey that cat is gone! Did you see it leave?"

"No", Margie replied. "Maybe we should go over and see if everything is alright."

Bill tried to dissuade Margie. "Nah, what could be wrong? You're making too much of an old man and his cat."

"Well why wouldn't he have told me if he had a new cat? I tell you, he was acting kind of strange last night. What would be wrong with going over to check on him? We can say we saw the cat and wanted to meet it."

Bill couldn't make a good argument against his wife's proposal so he reluctantly agreed to go along.

Sara had heard the noise and quickly ran down the hallway to the kitchen. Upon entering the room, she saw something and froze like a statue. Across the floor near the range was another mouse sniffing the underside of the stove. It didn't see Sara, but Sara's eyes could see nothing but the rodent.

The mouse had become totally absorbed in its fixation on the grease residue on the stove. Sara was able to move to her left, toward its rear and further into its blindside.

Sara calculated it was about six feet between

her and the mouse and she wanted to narrow that distance to four before she would lunge for the kill. The room was silent except for the tiny scratching noises the mouse was making. Sara's heart was beginning to beat faster and as she came within five feet of her prey, she opened her mouth, baring the incisors she would use for the kill.

She was moving in freeze frame motion now. She had him. Just one step away.

The pounding on the kitchen door broke the silence and the mouse scrambled away under the stove and ran back to a small hole in the baseboard. It was gone. Sara's tail puffed up and expanded to nearly twice its volume as she turned and raced out of the kitchen. Her fear of the unknown was quickly replaced with anger when she heard Margie's voice outside the door.

"Otis! You in there? Are you alright?" She had her head up to the window in the door and was trying to see inside.

Sara hissed from her hiding place under Otis's bed. "Go away bitch! You cost me my prey!" she growled in a low tone. She did not like humans all that well and she especially didn't like Otis's neighbor.

"I can't see anybody in there." Margie was telling Bill. "And he isn't coming to the door!"

"You said he had a rental car, maybe he decided to take it back himself this morning. Come on, let's go home."

Margie still strained to see through the window and continued to look.

"Yeah, he could have I guess," she finally said giving in to him. "I'll keep an eye out for him and see when he returns home."

Bill just shook his head. "I'm sure you will, Margie."

The two walked back to their own house. Margie kept looking back over her shoulder at Otis's kitchen door. She felt Otis might have been home but just pretended not to be. She hoped to maybe catch him watching them from the kitchen window as they walked away.. She didn't see anything, but she couldn't shake the feeling that something was different at her neighbor's house.

Jack Rand

The three men, Evert Dodge, Randolph Coats, and Otis Flagg who they knew as Jack Rand had ridden late into the day after leaving the station. It would soon be dark so they would have to stop and spend the night in the desert. Each on a horse, they had brought along a fourth horse as a pack horse to carry supplies. They were headed for a small cow town on the Rio Grande River called La Fuente. If the law came after them, they could cross the river into Mexico and be out of US jurisdiction. With any luck they would reach La Fuente tomorrow afternoon.

Otis had never ridden a horse before and yet was surprised at how quickly he adapted to riding in the saddle. The horse Dodge and Coats had brought along for him was a well behaved Mustang named Tanner. Otis learned that he had bought the horse two years earlier while up in Kansas. He had no memory of such a transaction, but had no reason to doubt it now. The horse never the less, was a beautiful light brown color that looked nearly tan in spots, thus his name, Tanner.
As they rode along Otis got the feeling that the horse knew and trusted him. It was a feeling Otis could somehow relate to.

The placed they stopped for the night was near a small stream where they could water the horses. Dodge estimated they had traveled twenty some miles and reminded Otis they had camped here before but out of respect asked, "Do you want to camp here for the night?"
Otis at first thought he was talking to Coats, before remembering that he was their perceived leader. "Yeah, we're a good day's ride from the station, let's camp here." Then

he added nonchalantly, "Where are we headed?"

Both men looked at him in disbelief before Coats answered him.

"Boss, I can see by your purple cheekbone, you must have been hit purty hard and it messed with your thought process. We're headed for La Fuente, you know, our hideout down on the border."

Otis touched his cheek and it was indeed sore, but it hadn't caused him to lose his memory or had it? Was he really the Otis Flagg he thought he was? He started wondering, thinking maybe he really was Jack Rand and the blow to the head from Burly caused him to think he was someone else. Surely this confusion he felt, would disappear as soon as they got to where they were going.

The men dismounted and began making camp by the stream in a flat area between a stand of cactus and sage brush at the base of a small rise. The sage brush grew in clumps surrounding them and would give them a generous break from the cold night winds of the desert.

Coats unsaddled his mare and went to work unloading the supplies the pack horse had carried. The sun had set and it would be dark soon. They would need a fire built not only to

warm their grub, but for warmth and light.
Otis wondered what there was to keep a fire
going out here in the desert, but didn't wonder
long when he saw Coats unload four or five
split fire logs from the pack horse.

Dodge got busy gathering dry brush for
kindling and within ten minutes, he was
building a fire in a small fire pit.

Otis surprised himself again when he
unsaddled his horse. He had never done this
before, but yet new how to do it with ease. He
would use his saddle as a pillow for his head
and as he carried it closer to the fire pit he saw
the initials JR for Jack Rand, burned into the
top of the leather saddle horn. Was he Jack
Rand or was he Otis Flagg? He asked himself
this question over and over and only became
more frustrated.

He reached a place by the fire and dropped his
saddle. Then out of nowhere the answer came
to him. He just might be both men.

"You okay boss?" Dodge was looking at him as
he knelt by the fire adding more kindling.
"You looked like you seen a ghost."

Otis smiled. "I just might have Dodge, but it
ain't gonna hurt us."

His inner turmoil had left him. He was Jack
Rand and Otis Flagg was a ghost living inside
him. He didn't fully understand, but he was
finally at peace with himself.

He went about going through his saddlebags

for clean socks when he came across the blue bottle. Why did he carry an empty blue bottle he wondered and then unwittingly he slid it inside a sock and pushed it to the bottom of the saddlebag. Perhaps it was for sentimental reasons.

The darkness of night covered them just as the campfire began flickering and creating shadows on their surroundings. The brush and tumbleweeds closest to them appeared to be dancing to and fro as the fire grew.

Coats had make a little makeshift grill out of a piece of wire fencing and was warming up a tin of beans.

"These beans will git you fartin' so if you don't want to get yer bedroll all stunk up, go easy." Coats said chuckling.

Dodge was sitting on his haunches across the fire from Coats. He spit out a chew of tobacco before replying, "You'd be the one to know 'bout fartin'. Your ass smells 'bout as bad as that shit grave we put that Bodie in."

Otis's ears picked up on the mention of Bodie, the man he called Burly. "I've been meaning to ask you fellas what you did with that Bodie. He was a big, mean son of a bitch. My cheekbone is still tender." Otis gingerly rubbed his cheek.

"Well boss, we didn't kill that bastard, but I'm sure he wished he was dead. Last we saw him

he was buried up to his chin in shit pudding."
Dodge's face took on the look of a smiling jack
o lantern in the flickering fire.
Coats laughed. "I never seen a fella swim in
puddin' before!"
Otis tried his best not to imagine the scene they
were describing even after what the man had
put him through. "Well hopefully he'll think
twice about hunting any of us down again."

A few minutes later Coats said the beans were
hot and Dodge stood up to get a tin dish out of
his saddlebags. Otis heard what he thought
was a popping sound from the crackling fire.
An instant later that noise was followed by a
loud splat sound. He looked up just in time to
see a huge red dot on Dodge's forehead before
he dropped exposing the bigger hole in the
back of his head. He had been shot from long
range by a huge weapon.

"Jesus Christ! Dodge's been shot!" yelled
Coats, scrambling to get his rifle laying next to
his saddle.
Otis pulled out his pistol and as Coats ran off
into the dark one way, he went the other, each
man heading in the direction of the gun shot.
The moon had yet to rise and it was very dark
away from camp. The sky was vast and thick
with stars, stars Otis had failed to see within
the light of the campfire. He realized he had

let the security of the campfire lower his guard and now once again he was being hunted.

He stayed low to the ground and moved very slowly, stopping every few steps to listen. The wind blowing through the brush made an eerie whistling sound that rose and fell sounding as if it was the breathing of a dying man.

He wondered where Coats was. He didn't want to be shot by him or shoot him by mistake. He had gone some thirty or forty feet from camp and decided to stay put until he could be sure of where Coats was.

Then a voice broke the silence.

"I've got you bastards now! Stand up and I won't kill you!" It was Burly and Otis wondered how that could be.

Then Coat's voice could be heard off to his left, "Fuck you Bodie! You killed Dodge! We should have drowned you in that shit hole!"

Otis could hear movement in the brush to his right.

"Yes, you should have you cocksucker! But you lost your chance and now I'm gonna blast you into hell! "

Otis started moving in the direction he thought the voice was coming from. Behind him the moon was rising and he knew that within the next few minutes they all would be able to see one another's positions.

When it became quiet once again he stopped

and listened and tried not to make a sound.
He feared his heavy breathing would give him
away.

Then twenty feet to his left he heard Coats yell
"There you are you giant son of a bitch!" And
he fired two quick shots from his rifle,
A moment passed and Otis heard Burly's
response.

"Eat these bullets!" And from where Otis
crouched he saw the burst of three shots being
fired and the silhouette of the huge man that
had fired them. Otis got up and rushed
toward the silhouette hoping to surprise him.

"Is that you Rand?!" Bodie shouted, turning
and pointing his rifle in Otis's direction.
Otis, holding his Colt.45 in one hand, quickly
fired off four rounds at the silhouette using the
heel of his free hand on the gun's hammer.
Bodie could only get one round off and Otis
felt it whiz past his right ear.

When Otis reached Bodie the moon had risen
high enough to shed light on the face of the
bounty hunter. The left side of his face was
missing, but he was still trying to speak. He
motioned Otis closer to his quivering mouth so
Otis could hear his last words.

Otis knelt down beside him and bent over him.
"What? What is it Bodie?

Bodie coughed and cleared some blood from
his throat, then in a hoarse whisper managed
to say one word, "Source."

It was like Otis's mind had been quick started. The source was his reason for being here! Memories came gushing into his mind. Memories of leaving Sara behind so he could find the gate keeper of time, to find the Source. Everything would fall into place once he found the Source!

Otis grabbed Bodie by the shoulders and shouted, "Where?! Who?! How do you know him?" So many questions he had. "How did you know I was looking for him? Are you him?!"

But the only sound was a gurgling in Bodie's throat. Then it stopped and his eyes became blank. Bodie had drowned in his own blood. Otis might have just killed the man that could have helped him. He was devastated.

Then from over his shoulder he heard Coats moaning. He stood up and in the dim moonlight, saw Coats lying about ten feet away. He was in bad shape, but he was still alive.

Otis was able to treat Coat's wounds and help him back to the campfire where the fire had simmered to embers. He threw the last log on the fire and shared the can of beans with Coats.

"You going to be able to ride in the morning?" Otis asked Coats, who had taken gun shots to his shoulder and hip.

Coats looked much older in the firelight than he did earlier. "I can ride, boss. We ain't got

that far to go to get to La Fuente. I can ride."
"Get some sleep then and we'll leave at sun up." Otis laid down and rested his head on his saddle. What a hell of a time period to live in, he thought to himself looking up at the moon. He longed to go back to Sara, but he couldn't go back just yet, not until he found what he was looking for.

Somewhere in the distance a coyote howled. That was the last sound he heard until day break.

Sara

Sara waited under Otis's bed until all was quiet once again. The nosy neighbors from next door had retreated back to their confines after spoiling her attack on a rodent intruder.

Her tail had now shrunk back to its normal size, whipping back and forth under the bed as she contemplated her next move. She came out from under the bed and trotted into the living room, heading for the windowsill. Jumping up she positioned herself behind the open curtain where she could spy on the neighbors.

Across the way she could see Margie moving around in her kitchen, stopping from time to time to look over at Otis's house. Sara did not like Margie. She had met humans like her before.

Her mind went back to her first day in this life. Back to when she came through the time portal in the cave. She was startled upon seeing herself as a feline and raced away from the cave into the ragged foot hills and right into the hands of the authorities. There behind a scraggly looking tree a human male had just finished urinating and managed to grab her as she ran by.

Try as she did, she could not break free from his grip and was carried down a trail to where he and his family were camped.

This was the Borders family, Christopher, Ellen, and their daughter, Sissy.

"Look what I found!" Christopher had declared coming into camp.

Sissy had looked up and her eyes became the size of silver dollars. "Daddy, can we keep it? Please! Please!?" She begged, holding her hands clasped as if in prayer.

Mrs. Borders had been against keeping her, but Sissy's pleading was too much for her Dad to say no. Sara, therefore was not only captured but claimed.

Her life with the Borders lasted for five years. Though not an awful existence, being torn away from a chance to get back through the portal and her human life, her life with her only son, had been crushing.

When she finally managed to escape, she navigated herself through dangerous mountainous terrain for months to finally return to her home in Rifle. There she found her son had grown up and had rented out the house they had shared.

Although she came to be in the presence of her son Otis, she could never communicate with him or allow him to know her secret. She lived a bittersweet existence. After he rented the house he moved away to Denver and left her with the couple that had become the renters. The Dunshees were an older couple who took good care of her and allowed her in and out of the house. But for some reason, unbeknownst to Sara they moved out six months later and left her behind. She pretty much had to fend for herself after that. She was forced to sharpen her hunting skills so as to get enough to eat until the day that Otis arrived looking for her. Now as she peered out from her hiding place behind the curtain, she hoped that Otis would return with good news, but even more importantly, she hoped he would return no matter what. She didn't want to be alone. She didn't want to have to battle the human female across the way. The one authoritarian that could make her life miserable.

Sara flicked her tail and flattened her ears as she watched Margie's window.

Jack Rand

Otis woke up at dawn and found that Coats had already saddled the horses and somehow had thrown Dodge's body across his horse's back for their ride into La Fuente.
"Jesus man, how did you do all of this in your condition? You should have awakened me."

Coats gave Otis an embarrassed smile. "I ain't hurt bad. No bullets kilt me yet. I figured you needed your sleep after gettin' your head bashed like you did and I owe you my life for killin' that giant of a bounty hunter, Bodie!"
Otis smiled and brushed the sand off his trousers. "You don't have to thank me, Coats. You and Dodge saved my life. Bodie was taking me to Butte Ridge to meet the hangman."
As soon as Otis told Coats this, his mind cluttered up and he couldn't remember how he knew about the hangman.
"That Bodie was an animal!" exclaimed Coats. "We left him drowning in a pool of shit back there and somehow he was able to get out of that shit hole, clean himself, saddle up, and ride all night to catch us. Why would anybody do that?"

Otis slapped his big brimmed hat against his leg and then put it on his head. "It was all for the money. In this world money and women can cause a man to do crazy things!"

Coats stood thinking about Otis's words. "I ain't never had much of either one."

"Cowboy, that's why you ain't crazy!" Otis gave Coats a broad smile. "Let's ride!"

He swung up onto his horse and Coats did the same. "What about the giant's body, we gonna just leave him?"

Otis looked over in the direction of Bodie's dead body. "We'll send the undertaker out from town to collect him. In the meantime the coyotes will keep him company."

They rode off heading south as the sun filled the sky just above the eastern horizon. Sometime later as the sun reached the sky overhead, they came over a small ridge and Otis got his first look at the wide valley that stretched out before them. They were about a mile away from La Fuente, the sleepy looking cow town that sat on the bank of the Rio Grande River. Otis knew that he was also looking into Mexico on the other side of the lazy stream and it gave him a feeling of safety.

"There it is Boss," Coats said as he stood in his stirrups to take some of the stress off of the bullet wound in his hip. "La Fuente, Texas!"

"That's a mouthful. How'd it get that name?" Otis asked, remaining seated in the saddle.

"Well the old timers say the river once flowed

on this side of town, so La Fuente was in Mexico to begin with. Then after a flood one year, the river changed course and stayed on the other side, moving the town to Texas."

" I like La Fuente. It is a beautiful Spanish name ." Otis remarked as he shook his reins, moving Tanner forward.

"Yeah, it sounds like a senorita's name and not the English name The Source." Coats added.

Otis nearly fell off his horse. "What did you say?!" His mouth was open in surprise.

"Did you just tell me La Fuente means the source in our language?"

"I am pretty sure it does. A senorita I knew told me that. I had no reason not to believe her. Is something wrong Boss?"

Otis remained silent and didn't answer. His mind was spinning with all sorts of thoughts.

Was this The Source Twirly had told him about? Was there some kind of God here? Surely he hadn't been talking about a town. Was this all a mistake? Had he gotten into a wrong parallel coming through the time portal? Twirly had to be talking about a special being of some importance and not a town.

The thought of returning through the portal immediately entered his mind. The blue bottle was in his saddlebag, he could go now, but he wasn't completely sure about what the source was. The only way to be sure would be to go into La Fuente. If he didn't, he'd never know for sure.

Coats had moved his horse up next to Otis so he could put a hand on his shoulder. "Boss, are you okay? You look like you might be sick."

Otis quickly came back to his present. "I'm gonna be fine Coats. My head wound still has me dizzy." He was telling Coats what he though Coats should hear. "Let's go. I want to get into town."

He kicked his spurs into the sides of his horse and Tanner lurched forward. Coats did likewise, pulling Dodge's horse along behind carrying the bouncing body of Dodge laying across his saddle.

Sara

Sara had left her hiding place in the living room window to visit her litter box in the basement. She hadn't seen any movement in the neighbor's window and had taken a cat nap before waking due to an urge in her bladder.

Otis had set up a wooden box for her in the basement and filled the bottom of it with kitty litter. She had gotten use to going outside, but this would work until Otis returned from visiting this source he was so excited about. The basement in Otis's house was more like a cellar to Sara's thinking. It was dark and cool and contained a smell that confused Sara's nose. The concrete floor was clean but Sara was careful where she placed her paws when she walked to the litter box.

She had no sooner finished her business when she heard a knocking upstairs at the back door again. Sara quickly covered her urine and ran to the wooden steps leading up to the kitchen. She jumped the six steps in two leaps and stopped on the landing where she crouched behind the door.

"Otis...Otis!"

The bitch is back! Sara hissed under her breath. Margie had indeed returned and this time she had brought with her the house key Otis had given her for emergencies. "Otis...it's me! Are you in there?!"

Sara heard nothing for a few seconds until there was the sound of a key in the back door lock.

Sara decided to stay where she was and hide behind the basement door.

The back door opened with a creaking noise and Margie stuck her head in and hollered out again. "Otis, are you here? Are you alright?!" When there was no answer Sara heard Margie come inside the house. The basement door was open just wide enough to let Sara move herself into a position behind the door to peer out between the door and the door frame.

Margie was standing in the kitchen, her eyes surveying the area.

Sara's first inclination was to jump out at Margie and scare her off, but experience had taught her that that could backfire and she would be caught immediately or hunted and captured. Either way she would be a prisoner of the authorities again. She waited silently behind the door as Margie walked through the kitchen and into the hallway.

"Otis!"

Margie searched the house and not finding Otis, came back into the kitchen where she eyed the basement door. She came over to the door and pushed on it gently. It made a creaking noise as it opened wider.

"Otis, you down there?"

When there was no answer, she stepped through the doorway and onto the landing.

"Otis!"

Sara was still behind the door, which now had been pushed open enough to pin Sara between the wall and the door. She raised her tail and it was expanding as she became more and more threatened. Margie felt along the wall for the light switch for the basement lights and upon feeling it, switched the lights on, flooding the

basement with dim light and shadows.
"Otis!?"
Margie didn't want to go down into the
basement, the result of watching too many
scary movies as a teenager. She lingered on the
landing, stretching her neck to see into the far
corners of the basement before switching the
light off. She backed herself into the kitchen
and closed the door, trapping Sara on the
basement steps landing.
Sara stood silent as she heard Margie let herself
out of the house before letting out a shrill
hissing sound. She was trapped. She could
only hope Otis would return soon.

Jack Rand

La Fuente was a small cow town of possibly
seventy inhabitants, mostly men. It had a main
street, two blocks long that supported various
businesses, many of which were dying after
the railroad failed to come through town three
years earlier, prompting families to move out.

There was a church and a school on one end of
town that had been left to decay in the brutal
sun. The church going people had all left town

and in doing so, took their children with them. Next to those two buildings stood the blacksmith shop and horse barn. The rest of the buildings on the main street were one and two story wooden buildings that were in need of repair.. There was the sheriff's office, one hotel, a hardware store, and three saloons, all of which boasted having the finest "ladies" north of the Rio Grande.. The town had become a destination for the vaqueros (Mexican cowboys), who rode in from across the Rio Grande most nights of the week. The town was wide open and had helped give the west, its wild reputation.

Otis and Coats rode in at a time in the afternoon when most of the town people were taking their afternoon siesta. It was very quiet. They rode down the dusty street and came to a stop in front of the blacksmith shop.

The horse barn with a corral behind it, was connected to the blacksmith building. Upon hearing Otis and Coats ride up, the blacksmith came outside into the mid day sun. Seeing Otis he stopped in his tracks and his face turned red as an apple.

"Jack Rand, they said you got hanged up in Butte Ridge!"

Otis looked down at the blacksmith. "They got it wrong. You got an undertaker here in town?"

The blacksmith had trouble swallowing.

"Nope, not any more. His wife shot him with both barrels of a double barreled shot gun last Friday after he was caught sneakin' out of Sweet Suzy's Fun Palace. If you need someone though, Eddie Morales has been filling in. He's most likely in one of the bars playing stud poker."

"Okay" Otis said, "we have a man here that needs buried. Then have him talk to Coats here, to get directions to another body about a half day's ride from here."

"I can do that." the blacksmith replied. "Anything else Mr. Rand?"

"Yeah, take care of our horses, they'll need feed and water for a few days. We'll be at the hotel and Coats will need someone to look in on him and don't call me Mr. Rand. It's just Rand."

The blacksmith bowed his head and took the reins of the horses as Otis and Coats hung their saddlebags on wooden pegs and walked toward the hotel.

It was about a block and a half to the hotel from the blacksmith shop and Otis was quick to notice that the three or four people they met on the way hurriedly ducked into stores or moved to the other side of the street when they recognized who he was.

"Looks like I'm still remembered around town." Otis said to Coats, who limped along beside him.

"Yeah, your face was posted all over 'round here a few weeks back. Everybody was talkin' about gettin' rich by bringin' you in."

Otis chuckled. "I saw the poster Bodie had, a thousand dollars is a lot of money. How come you never turned me in?"

Coats looked at Otis with wide eyes. "Cause you're the boss, boss. Besides that, I'm wanted myself up in Kansas."

"Oh yeah, how much is on your head?"

"Hundred dollars, the last I heard."

"Mm, maybe I'll turn you in!" Otis mused.

Coats made a funny facial expression and then grinned. "Shit boss, I'm worth way more than that just to watch your back."

"That you are Coats, that you are."Otis replied with a wink.

They reached the Maiden Hotel and went in. The lobby was empty. The only person in the room was the hotel clerk, a skinny little man with slicked back hair and wearing wire rimmed eye glasses. His black suit coat was wrinkled and in need of a cleaning. To Otis, the thing that stood out the most about the man was that he was sweating profusely.

Otis and Coats walked up to where the clerk stood behind the counter.

"Need two rooms, and I want mine overlooking the street." Otis said to the clerk.

The clerk placed a large registration book up on the counter. "It you gentlemen would sign this, I can take care of you."

"I ain't signin' nothin'!" exclaimed Coats.

"That's alright Coats, I'm doing the signing for both of us." Otis read down the names in the register and didn't recognize any of them. He then signed his name followed by Coat's.

The clerk who looked to be visibly shaken gave Otis and Coats their room keys.

"Would either of you gentlemen like me to send up one of our maidens to help you undress?"

"So that's how the hotel got its name?" Otis asked with the sternest of looks on his face.

The clerk began to shake. "I assure you Mr. Rand our ladies here are young maidens and not the kind of ladies you'll find in the saloons."

At that moment the door to the left of Otis and Coats flew open and in rushed a young gunslinger with a pistol in hand. He spoke to the clerk first.

"Good job Davidson, now get your ass out of here!"

"Please forgive me Mr. Rand." The clerk pleaded to Otis. "He threatened to kill me if I warned you."

"Go!" Otis told him and then turned to the

gunslinger. "Just who might you be and what do you want?"

The gunslinger couldn't have been more than twenty years old. His blue trousers were worn and his faded red shirt had a small tear under one arm. He wore a large white hat and as Otis focused on his face, he saw someone familiar. "I'm Bill Chesterfield, soon to be known as Billie Chester and you're gonna make me rich!"

"Don't do it cowboy." Coats said moving slowly away from Otis. "This here is Jack Rand and he'll kill you so fast, you'll wish you'd already been dead!"

The kid moved closer. "Is that right? He looks pretty old to me and old is slow. Jack Rand, you're worth a grand to me dead or alive. Get out on the street and I'll give you a chance to live."

"Have we met before?" Otis asked the cocky kid.

"Only in my dreams." The young gunslinger replied.

Otis finally recognized the face he was talking to. It was that of another Billie he had known, a younger Billie Cooper that had been the cabin boy that served him on a tall ship in another lifetime.

"Have you ever been to sea?" Otis continued to question him.

The gunslinger took on a look of bewilderment. "What kind of sea?"

"The ocean! Sailing around Cape Horn!"
The kid stood motionless thinking, then fired
his gun at the ceiling. "There ain't no ocean in
West Texas!" he yelled. "Now git outside!"

Otis and Coats slowly did as the kid ordered
and backed out of the hotel lobby and into the
street.
The kid had Coats throw his guns down in the
dirt before moving across the street and laying
down.
"Okay Rand, it's you and me. Keep your
hands where I can see them while I holster my
weapon, then we're gonna face off and draw,
you got that?"
Otis nodded his head and kept his hands and
arms out away from his body.
"Billie, you don't want to do this. You're too
young to die." Otis said in a steady voice. "We
have met before, you just don't remember."
"Quiet! Quit trying to confuse me! The kid
was slowly placing his gun in its holster.

Otis took a look around and saw they were the
only ones out on the street. Townsfolk were
watching from behind windows, but nothing
outside was moving in the hot sunshine.
The two men had taken their place in the
middle of the street and were facing each
other, standing about twenty feet apart.
Knowing Rand's reputation as a fast gun the

kid drew first, but it was never a contest. Otis drew and fired two rapids shots into the young man's body before the kid was able to raise his gun high enough to shoot. With a surprised look on his face, he fell into a slump. The faded red shirt he wore, soon took on a deeper shade of red as blood began soaking through.

Otis holstered his gun and walked up to the kid frowning and knelt down next to him. The young man's eyes blinked several times in disbelief as his breathing became labored. He looked up and seeing Otis a look of relief spread across his face. "Captn' Flagg, it's you." He smiled and his breathing stopped.

Coats got off the ground and walked over to where Otis was kneeling. "Boss, did you know him?"

Otis reached down and closed young Billie's eyes with his hand.

"No. The man I knew wasn't from these parts. This kid just reminded me of him, that's all. See to it that he gets buried will you?"

Otis stood up and walked back toward the hotel. Memories were running wild in his mind. His experience aboard the ship seemed a long, long time ago in another place, but then again he had learned that time wasn't linear, it's all around us at once. He realized he may have been on the ship moments ago and now he was here.

It was all too confusing for him to think about it right now. He had to concentrate on the task at hand, his being in his present state in a town called La Fuente. Was La Fuente where he needed to be? Would he find out what he needed to know to help Sara return to human form?

He stopped and looked around the cluster of buildings that made up La Fuente before entering the hotel. It was still quiet with no one moving about other than Coats, who was dragging the man he had just shot to the side of the street.

He entered the hotel lobby and if the clerk had returned, he was no where in sight. On the register counter lay his key, so he picked it up and climbed the staircase to the second floor, looking for room number 6. Room number 6 was near the end of the hall on the street side of the building. Otis unlocked the door and went inside.

Some things never change he thought. In the simple room was a single bed, with a wrought iron frame and head board. Next to it was a small wooden night stand. Across from the foot of the bed was the only curtain covered window. The walls were wallpapered with large white flowers on dark blue wallpaper. Otis went directly to the window and pulled back the curtain to look down at the street below. Coats had found two men to carry the dead gunslinger down to the undertaker's parlor and they were the only ones visible on the street.

Also in the room was a small table against the wall with a wash pan and pitcher of water. He flung his hat off and was about to wash some of the dust out of his eyes when there was a knock on the door.

Otis drew his gun. "Who is it?"

From the other side of the door came a female voice. "Jack Rand. I was told you might want to talk to me."

Otis moved closer to the door before answering. "Oh yeah? Just who told you that?"

"A cowboy that came through town last week, went by the name of Twirly."

Upon hearing Twirly's name Otis grabbed the door knob and flung the door open, surprising the woman in the hallway. Seeing the gun in Otis's hand caused her to cover her mouth with her hands. "Don't shoot!".

Otis saw that she was not armed and lowered his pistol. The Jack Rand in him had not seen such a lovely young woman in a very long time. Most saloon girls lived hard lives and the stress, wear, and tear of taking care of cowboys took its toll, but this young woman looked different. She looked almost like a real lady.

"I didn't mean to scare you." He said. "Come in." He stepped back to let her in the room and then bent forward to look out in the hallway to make sure there were no surprises.

With the door closed once again, he locked it and left the key in the lock and then turned to his guest.

Otis was having trouble keeping himself from staring at this woman. Her long whitish blond hair was tied up in what looked like a hundred curls and piled together high on top of her head. Her smooth cheek bones were powdered with light pink powder, accentuating two of the biggest blue eyes he had ever seen. When she wasn't talking her lips remained parted only to touch every few seconds as if she were pouting. She wore a blue and gold gown that Otis was sure was meant for the grand ballrooms of New Orleans or San Francisco. As they stood looking at each other, she held out her hand and introduced herself. "Hello, my name is Michelle."

Otis felt like a schoolboy. He wasn't sure if he should take her hand and kiss it or just shake it. He settled with just taking it and holding it for a brief few moments.

"Hello Michelle. You say you met a man named Twirly?"

Michelle smiled. "We actually got to know each other well in the short time he was here." Otis felt the schoolboy feeling again before regaining his composure. "What did he tell you about me?"

The smile left Michelle's face. "He told me you would be looking for something and that I might want to help you with."

Otis nodded. "Go on."

She moved to the window and looked out and skyward before turning back to Otis.

"I know you are looking for The Source and that quest led you here." She then came up to within inches of Otis's face and began to whisper.

"There is a time portal here and through that portal is what you seek."

With their faces so close, Otis felt like he was looking into her very soul.

"Will this portal allow me to return back here?" Otis was whispering now also. He didn't want to leave his blue bottle behind for it was his way back to Sara.

"Yes. I have the portal with me, but we must wait until the sun is setting. You will have ten minutes to pass through and return. Once the sun drops below the horizon, the portal will close."

Otis guessed the sunset was still three for four hours away. "I will have to wait then," he said more to himself than to Michelle.

Still inches away from each others face Michelle ended their conversation with a sly smile. Her lips had parted again and the tip of her tongue was dancing over her upper lip. Otis decided that waiting for sunset wouldn't be that bad after all and pulled the window shade down to block the intense sunshine flooding the room. The sun was making the room uncomfortably warm.

Sara

The cellar smelled musty. Sara hadn't noticed that, until Margie unknowingly locked her on the stairway landing. It was dark, but nothing that Sara couldn't handle. She only needed about one sixth the light a human needed to see. She could also sense motion in the near darkness, so she decided to do a little hunting. She crept down the wooden steps, stopping on each one to survey every nook and cranny.

The cellar consisted of one small room, ten by twelve feet at the most. Along one wall was a set of wooden shelves holding home canned fruit and vegetables. There were two rows of pint and quart sized Mason jars full of green beans, carrots, pickles, and tomatoes, from last summer's garden.

Sara guessed that this was the work of the nosy neighbor. It was true, she did look out for Otis, but Sara wondered if she didn't do it so she could control him.

On another wall was a crude work bench which looked to be used more as a catch all shelf than a work bench. There were two cardboard boxes filled with magazines on one end of the bench and numerous odds and ends sat on the other end. One wall was bare. This was the outer wall, the house foundation wall and just below where the house was attached to the wall was a narrow ledge, running the length of the wall. In the middle of the room, just above the ledge was a double paned basement window. Sara had not seen the window before and now it had her full attention. She jumped up onto the workbench and from there leaped up onto the ledge. She immediately encountered mouse droppings on the concrete ledge and guessed that the window was were the rodents were getting into the house.

She slowly crept along the narrow ledge until she came to the window. The outside of the glass was crusted with dust and dirt from seasons of neglect, which limited the amount of light coming into the cellar. The wooden window frame had rotted and decayed after years of spring and summer moisture. The putty that held the panes of glass in place was cracked and had broken free. Over time this had allowed a sizable chunk of glass to break and leave a hole big enough for mice to come and go.

Sara studied the hole and concluded it wasn't large enough for her to fit through. She hit the piece remaining in the frame with her paw. It made a noise, but didn't budge. She did it again and then again, to no avail. She was about to give up when she heard a loud growl from outside.

She backed away from the window as a huge dog attacked the noise Sara had been making. The dog's nose hit the loose pane of glass and it came crashing in on the top of the ledge.

The dog was crazy now, barking and digging at the window. Sara wasn't sure, but thought it must a Rottweiler. She was sure however that she must have pissed it off and was thankful it couldn't get at her.

"Bluto stop! Come boy!" The human voice was coming from outside. Sara could only surmise the dog belonged to the human or vice versa.

The dog stopped barking and growling, but before retreating whispered something to her in dog language, something she couldn't understand, being a feline.

Sara waited until she was positive the rottweiler had been taken inside, before creeping back to the window. The dog had done her a favor by knocking the window pane out of the frame. She could now get through the hole and outside.

Before making an escape, she peered out the window and could see that this side of the house was opposite the side the nosy neighbor lived on.

Sara looked around the cellar and then climbed through the window. She was free, at least for now.

Jack Rand

Otis could hear coughing coming from the next room. He had dozed off and was lying in his hotel bed. He realized he was alone and panic gripped him. Where had the woman gone!? He had been dozing and wondered for a few confusing seconds, if he hadn't dreamt her. Had there really been anyone in the room with him?

He looked at his pillow and his mind relaxed. There he saw a long strand of blonde hair. She was real! He jumped up and went to the window. The sun would set in the next thirty-five minutes and he remembered what she had told him. Time was of the essence. He had to find her. His fear was short lived. There was the sound of a key in the door lock and the door opened. Michelle let herself in and closed the door behind her.

"I was afraid you had gone." he told her in a low voice.

"I did go, but I'm back. Are you ready?" She was as beautiful as she had been earlier, but she had changed her clothes and was all business now. In place of her gown, she wore what to Otis looked like a pair of coveralls, something women of this era did not wear. She moved to the window and raised the shade. Out of her pocket she removed a solid green glass crystal that was in the shape of a resting frog and looked to be the size of an egg. Otis watched with great curiosity as she place the green crystal frog on the windowsill.

She looked out at the location of the setting sun and then at Otis. "When the sun lowers just a few more degrees in the sky, its rays will shoot through this crystal, opening a time portal in this room. When I tell you, move directly into the green rays and you will pass through."

"Are you coming?"

"No, I will stay here until you return. You must return before the sun gets too low and ceases to shine through the crystal."

"How much time will I have?" Otis was getting worried.

"You'll have enough time, but not enough to waste. Do you understand me?" She was dead serious.

Otis nodded his head and a moment later saw the first streak of green light from the crystal, shine into the room.

"Be ready!" Nora warned.

The reflected light from the glass frog grew more intense and then she yelled, "Now!"

Otis walked into the light and an instant later was bathed in light. Light so bright he was blinded by it.

"Otis Flagg?" a voice asked.

"Yes. Yes, I am Otis Flagg! Have I arrived? Is this the Source I seek?"

"Yes, I am the Source. I am the keeper of time and its movement.

"But it is so bright here, I can't see anything!." Otis covered his eyes.

"I'm nothing to see. I am only time and you are wasting me if you continue along this path. If you want to see time, you need only to look at your own refection in a mirror."

Otis continued. " I am here to ask for help for a friend."

"I'm listening."

"A very good friend of mine has become trapped in a different species. She entered a parallel life as a feline and due to no fault of her own, was unable to get back through the portal in time to return to her original state."

"And?" The voice asked.

Otis wasn't sure what to say. "That's it. Can you help?"

The Source was silent for what seemed to Otis like an eternity and then he spoke.

"There has been a wrinkle in time. The force

has shifted and your friend has come into her human existence again."

"Thank you! I am indebted to you."

"Go then and be careful how you use time. You may have to repay it."

Before Otis could reply, he felt a surging wind and felt himself being pushed backward. The bright light he had experienced was turning green and all of a sudden he was back in his hotel room where Michelle was waiting.

As soon as Otis was clear of the green rays of light, she took his place and entered the portal. He saw her wave goodbye and ten seconds later the sun slipped over the horizon and the green rays from the crystal frog evaporated. The portal had vanished, taking her with it. Otis picked up the green crystal frog and held it in his hand. It was warm. He wondered if he was to take it with him or leave it. He reasoned that he was to keep it and put it in his pocket. Having finished his business here he went to look for Coats. Otis wanted to get back to the horse corral and his saddlebag where the blue bottle was. He was eager to return to the present time and Sara..

Sara

Sara had never been on the north side of the house. The basement window was on the north side and she had always either spent time in the window in the living room or in the kitchen, where the door to the backyard was. Both faced south.

After coming out though the basement window she trotted to the backyard and into the sunlight. The backyard was not that big but had become one of Sara's favorite places. There was an apple tree close to the house and one of Sara's favorite pastimes was watching the fluttering birds in the tree's branches.

The birds always seemed to know when she was watching them. They could see her sitting in the windowsill, her tale whipping, and hear her making a distinct chattering sound. As they fluttered about, there was never any fear, not as long as she was inside the house.

They didn't see her slowly stepping around from the north side of the house. They had never seen her outside, let alone on the north side out of the sun

.

Sara heard them chirping and fluttering as she approached the corner of the house and crouched low, keeping herself as close to the house's foundation as she could. Peering around the corner she let her eyes drift upward and settle on one of the lower branches where a pair of grosbeak finches sat singing and rubbing beaks.

Sara hadn't had bird for quite a while and the thought of fresh finch started her tail waving very slowly and methodically. She plotted her strategy and every move she made in the next minute would be made with precision and cunning. She took a step forward out of the shadows and stopped. The birds were oblivious to her presence. Their joyful singing was probably being heard by and delighting the old woman that lived a few houses away. To Sara it was cause to salivate. One more step and she would be close enough to leap.

As she lifted her paw to move, the silence ended. The finches flew away in panic as Sara turned to see Bluto, the rottweiler a mere three feet away, almost upon her. His teeth glistened with saliva and his crazed eyes were focused on nothing but her fury body.

Sara shot out of her crouch, tail raised and full. She darted around the back of the house and up the driveway between Otis's and Margie's houses. The huge dog was growling and snapping right behind her. He was so close she could hear his dog tags jingling on his collar. From what seemed like miles away Sara thought she could hear the dog's owner yelling for the dog to stop, but Bluto didn't want any part of stopping. He wanted a cat, this cat! Sara managed to pull ahead as she reached the end of the driveway and darted into the street. She never saw the delivery truck. It hit her and she was flung high into the air, coming down with a thud on the far side of the pavement. Everything went sideways and she lost consciousnesses.

The rottweiler stopped short of the street and looked around, not sure of what had happened. His human came running up from behind him shrieking his name. "Bluto! Get home!"

The dog turned and took off running back to its property, his owner followed close behind. The finches had returned to the apple tree and took up where they had left off. They felt safe again. The cat was nowhere in sight.

Jack Rand

The sun had set in La Fuente and as Otis came out of the hotel he found that the sleepy town had come awake. With the work day over, cowboys were riding into town and filling up the saloons. There was laughter punctuated with a gunshot fired into the air every few minutes. Piano music was coming out of the saloon across the street and he could hear women laughing and men yelling.

Otis hadn't found Coats in his room and figured he would find him drinking whiskey at one of the three watering holes or maybe taking out his urges with one or two senoritas up the stairs.

Otis crossed the street and went into the Silver Saddle Saloon. The piano was louder inside as a gang of vaqueros celebrated the end of a cattle drive. There looked to be two women for every man and Otis hadn't made it three steps in the door when a red haired miss grabbed his arm. Her dark hair was piled high and full of a cheap perfume smell. Her face had been painted to accentuate her dark eyes and her pursing lips which were painted cherry red.

"Hey cowboy, you looking' for a good time?"

Otis tried pushing her away.

"Not tonight, darlin', I'm looking for someone."

The woman pushed her lips out in a pout.

"You just found her. I'll make you forget who you're looking for."

Otis moved on past her and she quickly latched on to the next cowboy coming through the doorway. At the bar Otis asked the bartender if a wounded cowboy had come in, a cowboy with a shoulder wound and a wound to the hip.

The bartender shook his head no and Otis left just as a fight was breaking out behind him.

Out on the street he turned to walk down to the next saloon five doors away. As he walked, a gang of cowboys came riding into town. He counted eight men on horseback and it wasn't until they stopped their horses across the way that he realized it was a posse. They had stopped in front of the sheriff's office and were talking loudly as they dismounted.

He wasn't sure if it was him they were after, but in the twilight he felt quite sure they hadn't seen him well enough to be recognized. Otis slunk back against the wall and stayed in the shadows. He watched two men from the bunch go into the sheriff's office while the others stood outside, two or three of them relieved themselves in the street.

Not sure of what to do next, he decided to cross the street and try to get a look inside the sheriff's office to see what he could learn. He walked slowly across the street acting like he had had too much to drink. His hat was low over his face and no one in the posse paid him any attention.

As the cowboys talked among themselves, Otis walked up and looked into the sheriff's office window. One of the men talking to the sheriff wore the badge of a US Marshal and Otis froze when he saw the wanted poster he was showing the sheriff. It was the same poster the bounty hunter had showed him only now Jack Rand was worth $1500 dead or alive! The sheriff looked surprised and was pointing toward the hotel when Otis backed away from the window. He had to get out of town and fast. He wouldn't be able to find Coats now, he had to leave and hoped Coats would understand.

He knew the Marshal and Sheriff would head for the hotel to look for him and that would give him time to get back to the blacksmith and horse corral. He took off walking but not so fast to bring attention to himself. He was thankful for the darkness that had fallen and kept moving.

Across the street from him the piano player in the Silver Saddle was playing a ragtime riff so loud that even the waiting members of the posse started jumping up and down in the street. Otis wondered if this is how the phrase "dancing in the street" came about in later years, but kept moving toward the corral.

The blacksmith's shop was dark except for the light coming from the window above the shop where the blacksmith lived with his wife. Otis kept looking back over his shoulder, but no one had followed him yet. As he slipped past the blacksmith shop and came to the corral, he saw the blacksmith step out of the shadows. He was holding a shotgun.

"I wouldn't go any farther, Rand. You're

worth as much dead as you are alive and to me, I could give a fuck. The Marshal will be here soon and I'll be a rich man!"

Otis did not move, but pleaded with the blacksmith. "You all think I'm Jack Rand, but I'm not."

"Is that right? Then just who are you? Your man was here earlier and rode out. He said you was Jack Rand. Why would he lie?"

Otis was awestruck. "Coats was here and then left!?"

"Yep. Got word the Marshal was headed this way. Said he couldn't find you. He's probably across the river and half way to Los Locos by now."

The little Mexican village of Los Locos struck a cord in Otis's mind. It was fuzzy to him, but as Jack Rand he had a hideout near there.

Otis felt defeated. He thought about rushing the blacksmith, but the double barreled 12 gauge shotgun aimed at him had him refrain from such action. He'd never get to him before being blown away.

He heard voices coming up the wooden sidewalk. The blacksmith hollered out, "Up here Marshal! I got Jack Rand up here!"

The gang of men came running down the boardwalk, guns drawn and surrounded Otis and the blacksmith. When the Marshal got close enough to see Otis's face he smiled and looked at the Sheriff.

"Sheriff, send somebody for Judge Black and set up a trial for tomorrow. Looks like we're gonna have us a hangin'!"

Everyone in the crowd began cheering. Everyone except Otis Flagg.

Sara

The delivery truck driver was on Otis's street to deliver someone a new mattress and had taken his eyes off the road to look down and check his directions. He never saw Sara. What startled him was the dull thud he felt in the steering wheel. He looked up and saw something land off to his left and stopped immediately.
He jammed the parking brake on and turned on his emergency flashers before jumping out of the truck's cab.
"Oh my God!" he said out loud as he saw the body lying motionless on the side of the street. He saw people coming out of their houses and he yelled, "Call 911...somebody call 911!"

Margie saw the commotion in front of her house and was one of the first ones to join the truck driver.
She saw the body of the woman in the street and her heart started pounding what seemed like two hundred beats a minute.

"I never even saw her, she came out of nowhere."The driver said, his voice cracking.

"Take it easy young man." Margie told him as she crouched down next to Sara.
In the distance the sounds of sirens filled the air. Margie reached down and placed her fingers on Sara's neck to feel for a pulse.
She looked up at the driver. "She's still alive. The ambulance will be here soon." She then turned to Sara and said in a soothing voice. "Hang in there honey, help is on the way."
That afternoon in the Princeton Lake Journal the following story made the front page:

YOUNG WOMAN HIT BY DELIVERY TRUCK

A young unidentified woman was struck by a delivery truck today as she crossed 11th Street. The driver of the Joyful Sleeper truck, Zak Prescott,46, of Rockwell, MN. told the investigating officer that the woman came out of nowhere. After passing a sobriety test, no charges were filed.
The woman was transported to the Jackson Medical Center Hospital where her condition is listed as critical. The woman carried no identification on her and authorities are asking for help in identifying her. She is listed as Caucasian, with dark hair, about 5'6", 120 lbs., and approximately 25 to 30 years old. Anyone who may have information about this woman is asked to call the Police Tip Line at 800-555-TIPS.

After the accident Margie had checked to see if Otis was at home. She thought it strange that he hadn't come outside when the ambulance was there with its lights twirling and flashing. She was beginning to worry about his absence. She knocked three times on his front door and when there was no answer, went around to the kitchen door. Satisfied that he wasn't home, she walked back to her own place and went inside. She would keep an eye out for his return.

Jack Rand

The La Fuente jail house was a small two room building in the middle of the block with the office in the front and two jail cells in the rear. Otis had been taken by the US Marshal and the La Fuente Sheriff and locked in the smaller of the two cells. Not long after Otis had been incarcerated, the sheriff brought in and jailed a Mexican cowboy who had drank too much at one of the saloons. Otis later learned that he had thrown a half bottle of whiskey at the mirror behind the bar causing it to shatter and crash down on the bartender, nearly cutting off one of his ears.
The Mexican vaquero physically fought his captors and continued to scream obscenities at them in Spanish long after they left him in his cell.

Otis waited until the drunken cowboy finally settled into a drowsy stupor before he tried to get some sleep, but he had too much on his mind.

Otis had been close to reaching his saddlebag and as he lay in the jail cell bunk, he could see it hanging on a peg in the horse barn. He hoped no one thought they needed it or become curious and start nosing through it, finding the blue bottle. If anything happened to the bottle, any chance of his escaping this place and time would be hopeless. He would be in this time forever and forever would be short.

It didn't look good for him no matter what. In the morning there would be a kangaroo trial and he would be hanged at noon.

He guessed the time to be somewhere around ten o'clock. From his barred cell window he could hear a saloon piano playing and women laughing. Every now and then someone would fire a gun and everything would get quiet for five or ten seconds before the noise and laughter started again.

Just as Otis was beginning to doze off he heard the Mexican in the next cell whispering something to him.

"Rand, ¡estoy aquí para ayudarte a escapar! Coats vendrá pronto con hombres y caballos!"

"I don't speak Spanish. English, English!" Otis

whispered back with a sense of urgency. The cowboy repeated himself in English.

"I'm here to help you break out! Coats is coming soon with men and horses!"

The two men were both now face to face with only cell bars separating them.

"Coats is coming? When?! Otis asked.

"Soon. Midnight. He will pull the bars from the windows and get us out. We will be across the river in no time!"

The cowboy grinned beneath a thick black mustache. "Tomorrow we will drink tequila and if they come after us, we will piss on their graves!"

Otis felt a glimmer of hope. As they waited they spoke in hushed tones and Otis learned that Coats had sent the Mexican to get thrown into jail to alert him to the escape plan. The Mexican vaquero's name was Manuel and after their short time as cell mates, Otis had a feeling they had met before, which would have been impossible in his current life. He let the feeling simmer in the back of his mind. Perhaps it would come to him later, but for now he had a much bigger concern and that was retrieving his saddlebag from the horse barn.

He asked Manuel, "Once we get out of here, is there a way we can get to the horse barn? My saddlebag is there."

"Senior Rand," Manuel replied, "You can have

ten new saddlebags when we get to Los Locos!
Don't worry about this old one. Saddlebags
they are like senoritas, when they old you get a
new one!" He was smiling broadly, showing a
mouth full of teeth.
Otis couldn't help but smile at Manuel's
boastfulness.
"You have a point my friend, but my
saddlebag is different. It holds something very
dear to me."
Manuel thought for a moment then shook his
head in agreement and with a wink said, "
Aah, this one is special. Not to worry Rand, I
will get it for you myself. You ride with Coats
and the others and I will catch up with you,
Si?"
Otis smiled and shook his head. "Gracias!"

Just as the men got back to sitting on their own
bunks, the wooden door between the office
and the jail cells opened and a deputy came
though.
"It's awful fucking noisy! You two hombres
having trouble sleeping back here?"
Otis could tell the deputy had been drinking
by the way he talked to them.
Otis quickly answered so Manuel wouldn't get
into an argument with the deputy.
"That was just me praying! Can't a man that's
going to swing from the gallows tomorrow
pray before he dies?"

The deputy wasn't expecting that answer. He stood weaving and blinked his eyes as if he were trying to remember something.

"Well don't pray so god damned loud then. I need to get some sleep so I don't miss watchin' you swing tomorrow!" He laughed heartily out loud as if he was proud that he thought of a response, then he turned and left Otis and Manuel in the dim cell room.

"I'd like to put a knife in his belly." whispered Manuel, "and then watch him laugh."

At midnight, Otis heard the sound of someone at his cell window.

"Boss! You in there?" It was Coats.

Sara

Sara opened her eyes in the ICU at the Jackson Medical Center Hospital. At first her eyesight was blurry before slowly coming into focus. She was lying in a bed surrounded by machines, each producing a sound, but all in unison. Her consciousness alerted a nurse fifteen feet away at the ICU nurse's station. She stopped what she was doing and came to Sara's side.

The nurse made a quick check of the machines monitoring Sara's vitals and then looked at Sara's swollen face and smiled.

"Hello. Don't try to talk." the nurse held a hand held device and made some entries with her finger. "We want you to rest, OK? Just blink once for yes and twice for no."

Sara focused her eyes on the nurse and blinked once.

"Okay, you're going to be alright honey. Just rest. We'll take care of you."

Sara closed her eyes and let herself drift back to the blackness.

Jack Rand

Otis stood up and looked out the cell window. The window was 2 feet high by 3 feet long with four black steel bars embedded into the rock wall at the top and bottom, about 6 inches apart. "Coats, I'm here!" Otis said in a loud whisper. "Manuel is in the other cell."

"It won't be long. We'll have you out pronto, as soon as we take care of the deputy."

Otis was about to ask what the plan for that was when he heard two muffled gun shots come from the office. A second later the door from the office opened and another vaqueros enter the cell room.

"It's done, he'll be sleeping for a long time." the cowboy said

Upon hearing this, Coats put a large braided rope in and around the bars of Otis's window. From there the rope was connected to a team of horses standing some ten feet from the building.

"Stand back Boss." Coats advised and the horses took up the slack in the rope. It didn't take much effort on their part as the stone walls were dry and porous. The bars were easily pulled free of their setting in the stone and after freeing Otis, the process was repeated for Manual.

Coats had brought six men with him and two extra horses for Otis and Manuel.

"Coats, I'm gonna need my saddlebag from the horse barn." Otis said as they mounted the horses.

"Boss, that will be too risky. The posse that rode in tonight is bunked there instead of the hotel."

Manuel broke in. "I can get it for him. They don't know me and think I just rode in myself."

Coats looked at Otis. "It's up to you boss, but we should ride before someone sees that you've escaped. Manuel can catch up with us on the other side of the river."

Otis looked at Manuel. "You sure Manuel? If not, we can hit them before they know what's going on."

Before Manuel could answer they heard a gun

being fired into the air in the front of the sheriff's office. This was followed by a yell, "There's been a jail break! They killed the deputy and escaped!"

To add to the hollering, someone started ringing a bell repeatedly.

" Son of a bitch!" Manuel yelled.

"Coats, take the men and ride. I'll catch up with you!"

"Boss, we are coming with you! There is no time to waste! Everyone will go running to the sheriff's office and not expect us at the horse corral."

Otis agreed. "We can set their horses free while we are at it!"

They rode from behind the sheriff's office and kept behind the buildings that lined the street. The corral was not that far and they could hear the bell continue to ring behind them.

Otis and Coats reached the corral first and saw the last of the posse members running toward the sound of the bell. They dismounted and ran into the barn as Manuel and the other men worked to open the gate and free all the horses. Luckily there was a lantern lit and hanging in the center of the barn spewing a bright glow creating irregular shadows on the walls.

Otis looked at all the walls but didn't see his saddlebag hanging anywhere.

"Shit! Someone took it!" he exclaimed.

"Is this what you're looking for?"   The

blacksmith had entered the barn holding the double barreled shotgun. He had thrown the saddlebag on the floor in front of him.

Otis looked at the saddlebag then at the blacksmith's face.

"Yes. It's mine. Let me have it and we'll be gone, no one will get hurt."

"I don't think any of you are going anywhere." The blacksmith had raised the shotgun up to where it was pointed at Otis and Coats. His face was full of contempt.

"I sent the woman for the sheriff."

Otis watched the look in the blacksmith's face change from contempt to surprise.

"Sorry amigo, but your time is up." It was Manuel who had come up behind the blacksmith and put a hunting knife into his back. The blacksmith dropped the shotgun and then dropped to his knees, where he balanced momentarily before falling forward on his face.

"Come, there is no time to waste!" Coats said touching Otis on his shoulder.

Otis picked up his saddlebag and hurriedly looked inside. There it was! The blue bottle still corked and wrapped in a sock.

He looked at Coats and said, "My friend take the men and go, go quickly. I will stay behind long enough to keep them busy while you make it across the river."

"No boss! We can not leave you here alone,

you must come with us!

In the distance could be heard the sound of men running on foot toward the horse barn.

"Coats, go! That is an order!"

Coats and Manuel looked at Otis not sure of what to do.

"Go, God dammit!" Otis yelled.

The two men quickly mounted their horses and before riding out, Coats hollered, "We'll see you on the other side!"

"Yes, the other side." Otis promised.

He waited until he was sure they had made it to the river to get the blue bottle out of his saddlebag. As the sheriff and the Marshall entered the barn with guns drawn, Otis removed the cork from the bottle.

He wasn't there to see their looks of disbelief when he vanished before their eyes.

Sara

Otis awoke moments later somewhat groggy in his easy chair. He tried to remember how long he'd been dozing. Sometimes when he napped too long, he woke up feeling worse than before he'd gone to sleep. This was one of those times. Even his heart rate seemed rather fast for slumber, suggesting bad dreams.

He stood up and looked out the window. The late afternoon shadows of trees were stretching out between his and the neighbor's house. He had slept longer than he had wanted to and it upset him. Too much sleep was a waste of time and time was too precious to waste.

Otis headed to the bathroom to relieve himself and as he did so, began getting flashes of memories. Memories just outside his realm of remembering them or what they were about. They might have something to do with the blue bottle, but he couldn't quite recall.

As he finished his duty and pulled up the zipper on his trousers, he felt something in his right pocket. Reaching in, he felt the smooth green crystal frog and his head exploded with the memory of his Jack Rand episode.

He nearly fell back into the bathtub, catching himself by grabbing on to a towel rack.

He looked at himself in the bathroom mirror and he was white as a sheet.

Feeling the green crystal frog was like hitting a nerve connected directly to his memory. It had been on the windowsill to catch the rays of the sun and within those green rays was a time portal to The Source! His plan had been successful. He had been able to do something about Sara. Sara!

He excitedly ran out of the bathroom yelling, "Sara! Sara! I'm back, where are you?!"

Otis searched the house, but she was nowhere to be found. Going down into the basement he saw the broken pane of glass in the window above the ledge and feared the worst, Sara had gotten out and gotten lost or hurt. Maybe she had given up on him and run off somewhere. Otis's heart rate was now accelerated more than before.

He climbed out of the basement and let himself out the back door. "Sara!"

Next door Margie was getting things ready to prepare supper when she heard Otis calling out for someone. She looked through the window and seeing him, stopped what she was doing.

She called to her husband, "Bill, Otis is back! He's out in his back yard looking for someone. I'm going over to see if he is alright."

"For Christ's sake Margie, leave the old man alone why don't you." Bill was frowning in his favorite chair.

Margie was already out the back door. "Otis, yoo-hoo!"

Otis saw her and his heart sank. What had he talked to her about the last time he saw her he asked himself. It soon came back to him.

"Otis, I've been watching for you all day. I came over earlier and you weren't here. Bill and I have been worried sick."

Otis feigned a smile. "Oh hi Margie! No need to worry about me. I took the rental car back to the rental place and then took one of those Uber rides home." He wished he'd never befriended this woman. She could be worse than an old mother hen.

"Well I wish you would have let us know. I was afraid you might have fallen down in your house and you know, couldn't get up."
"Margie, you worry too much sometimes."
Otis wanted to bring this conversation to an end, but Margie wasn't about to let that happen quite yet.

"Too bad you had to leave Otis, you missed all the excitement here earlier today."
"What kind of excitement?" Otis did his best to act like he was really concerned.
"Some poor young woman got hit by a delivery truck, right out in front of your house. It was terrible!"
Otis stopped acting and became genuinely concerned. "Who was it? Is she alright?"

Margie savored being the bearer of news and she could tell she had Otis's full attention now. "The ambulance and paramedics got here in no time and loaded her up. She was still alive when they took off, sirens blaring. It's just like on the TV news! In fact I think they were here!"
"Do they know who she was?" Otis asked again. He was starting to put two and two together, thinking of his conversation with The Source and his promise to alter time so Sara could regain her human self again. Could that

be what all this was about?

Margie's mouth was still moving. "The young woman didn't have any identification on her, no purse, billfold, or anything. The last I heard she was being called Jane Doe."

Otis stood waiting for her to stop rambling then asked. "Where did they take her?"

"Jackson Medical Center. I thought you knew that. That's where they take everybody in this area." Margie said with her hands on her hips.

"I didn't know that, but I'll write that down Margie, thanks."

They talked for a few more minutes and Otis was finally able to get free. Margie went back into her house and Otis his.

He immediately went into the study and opened his laptop to start searching for information on the accident Margie had just described.

It took him a bit of searching but he soon found the local newspaper's website and found the story as it had been released.

WOMAN HIT BY TRUCK CLINGS TO LIFE

The young woman hit by a delivery truck this morning has been put into medically induced coma while doctors work to save her life. The woman is Caucasian, with dark hair, about 5'6", 120 lbs. and approximately 25 to 30 years old. Her identity remains a mystery and the police are asking for help in identifying her. They ask anyone with information about her to call the accident tip line..1-800-555-TIPS.

Otis re-read the woman's description then sat back in his chair. He thought this woman sounded too young to be Sara. That would have been Sara's age back on the raft trip. His mind became cloudy. That would have been her age on the raft trip, but when was that? Thirty years ago or thirty minutes ago in another time dimension?
He hit his fist on the desk with a thud and gritted his teeth. He was going to have to get in to see this woman in the hospital. He had to make sure it wasn't Sara. If it wasn't her, he had to start looking for her. She was out there somewhere still a feline and fending for her life. He hit the desk again. He was getting too old for this!

The sun had set and Otis had to get out of the house without Margie seeing his departure. He contacted Uber and asked that the driver meet him on his street corner. Fifteen minutes later he was in the back seat of a Chevy conversion van heading for the hospital.
The driver, a young man in his twenties, in making conversation asked Otis if he'd ever been in a conversion van before. Otis smiled and after a pause, answered, "Boy I don't

know, it's been a while."

Ten minutes later they pulled into the entryway of Jackson Medical Center and Otis got out and entered the hospital.

Directly inside the door was the information desk staffed by a smartly dressed middle aged woman.

Seeing Otis approach, she smiled and greeted him.

"Welcome to Jackson Medical Center. How may I direct you?"

Otis had put on a dress shirt and clean trousers for the visit and nodded his head to the woman after she spoke.

"Hello. My name is Otis Flagg and I'm here to see the young woman who was hit by the truck this morning."

The woman's smile disappeared as she gave Otis a more serious look. "Do you know who she is, Sir?"

"Well, I won't know for sure until I see her." Otis replied, trying to look as innocent as he could.

The woman's smile returned and she asked him to please wait a moment.

Otis took a seat in the waiting area and a couple of minutes later he was approached by someone Otis guessed was a doctor or at least a hospital employee.

"Mr. Flagg?" the woman asked.

"Yes, that's me."

"I'm Doctor Mills, but please call me by my first name, Ann.

Otis stuck out his hand to shake hers. "Nice to meet you, Ann. Please feel free to call me Otis."

Otis couldn't get over how the female gender were taking over all the professions that had been filled mostly by men in his day. He was living in a new era.

"Alright Otis. What can you tell me about our Jane Doe in ICU?" Ann had come right to the point.

Otis wasn't sure how to begin. "Well, I've been away and when I returned today, I found that my good friend Sara was missing. When I read the story about this poor young woman hit by a truck, I wondered if maybe it wasn't my friend.

Doctor Mills looked at Otis intently as if she were deciding if she should believe him or not.

"Okay Otis. I'm going to take you back to ICU so you can see her. She is in a comma so we can't stay long, but hopefully you'll be able to make an identification."

Otis nodded and he followed Ann through the double doors and into a hallway that led to the ICU. Along the way she handed him a hospital mask to put over his nose and mouth.

A short distance later they passed through

another set of double doors into the ICU of the hospital. There were four different room modules positioned in a semi-circle around a nurse's station that looked to Otis like it could be the control area of a spaceship. Round colored button shaped lights flashed and blinked next to dials, gauges, and switches. Each room module had a hospital bed in the center, attached to various other machines with blinking lights and lighted gauges. There were two nurses on duty in the control center and they paid little attention to Otis and the doctor. He was taken to the first module where the accident victim lay connected to a patient monitor, a digital blood pressure monitor, an anesthesia machine, and two other high tech medical devices Otis didn't recognize. He was intimidated, but tried not to show it and moved up close to the bed.

His heart skipped a beat, he was looking at Sara! She lay there, eyes closed, her face slightly swollen with black and blue bruises. An oxygen tube was affixed to her nose and a heart monitor that monitored her every heart beat.

It was Sara the way she looked when he first met her long ago in Glenwood Springs. He was shaken by seeing her this way, but hid his reaction to Doctor Mills as he stared down at Sara.

"Well," Anne said. "Do you recognize this

person?"

Otis looked at Anne. "No. This is not my missing friend."

They left the ICU and Doctor Mills walked with Otis back to the main entrance.

"Well Otis, I hope you find your friend."

"Thank you Doctor. I'm sure she'll turn up. I just feel bad for that young woman back in the ICU. What will happen to her?"

"Oh when she comes out of her coma, we'll help her find out who she is. She'll get good care."

"I'd like to help." Otis said. "If she needs a friend, I'd like to volunteer to help her."

Anne smiled. "That would be wonderful Otis. Give the nurse at the station your phone number and we'll call when Jane Doe is awake and wanting company."

"I'll do that." Otis said happily.

Doctor Mills left Otis standing by the entrance station, where he gave the nurse his phone number and left.

Outside, Otis walked to a nearby taxi stand and got a ride home. His mind was full of questions. Did this happen because of his meeting with the Source? Because she had looked so young, would she still be the same person? Would she even know him? Would this affect their relationship?

How did it happen that she would be hit by a truck?

These were all questions that would be answered once she was awake and they were together again.

The bigger question at hand was how he would get her out of the hospital. He wasn't a relative. She had no medical insurance, she didn't even have an ID.

Otis had the taxi drop him off down the street from his house. He didn't want Margie or Bill see him and wonder what he'd been up to. His life had become too complicated as it was.

A week passed and it seemed to be one of the longest weeks Otis had ever had. Even waiting for Christmas as a child hadn't lasted this long he told himself one morning as he drank his coffee.

He monitored daily news on the Jackson Medical Center website and searched for any word on Sara's condition.

There was often generic updates without giving out confidential information about patients and Otis had taught himself to read between the lines.

Finally eight days after the accident, he saw what he was looking for. Posted at the bottom of page one was this bit of news:

Hospital ICU empty for the first time in 12 weeks.

Otis blinked his eyes and read it again. The

ICU was empty, meaning Sara was in a recovery room. She must be awake!

He finished the last of his coffee and called a cab to pick him up in 30 minutes. As he showered he formulated a plan for finding her room and getting in to see her without anyone knowing.

Thirty minutes later a cab driver was sitting out front of his house in a cab. Otis walked out his door and saw Margie watching him from her window. He did the neighborly thing and gave her a goodbye wave and moved toward the waiting taxi. He knew this would just be driving her wild and he couldn't help but smile to himself.

A short drive later Otis had the driver drop him off near the rear of the hospital, where he knew the hospital would receive most of its food deliveries. He had worked in food service as a younger man and knew what he was looking for.

Otis wanted to wear something white so he dressed in an old faded white milk man uniform he had worn years ago to a Halloween party.

He had always known it would come in handy someday and today was that day.

He waited around outside trying to be inconspicuous and luckily didn't have to wait for long. Pulling off the street and into the parking lot of the hospital delivery dock came a **Sysco** food delivery truck. Otis waited as the driver backed into the dock and began to unload before he made his move. As the driver and hospital receiving employees engaged in checking in product, Otis walked in and slipped by them unnoticed.

From the receiving area he entered a hallway that led to the vast hospital kitchen.

Here it began to get noisy as pots and pans clanked and huge boilers intermittently let off spurts of steam while cooking. Along one wall near the entrance where Otis stood was a rack of clean kitchen uniforms. This is what Otis was after. He walked right in and up to the rack, acting as if he was a kitchen employee. He quickly searched through the uniforms until he found one his size and removed it. He looked over his shoulder and was relieved to see no one paying attention to him. He took the uniform into a nearby washroom and when he came back out, looked just like the other fifty or so people running around the kitchen area.

He had made it in, now he needed to find out what room Sara was in. He picked up a small rack of clean silverware from a shelf and started walking to what he perceived was the kitchen office. It was nearly 10 AM so the push for the noon meal was now in progress. The kitchen manager was standing at a workstation sorting a stack of papers when luckily for Otis, she was called away to the far end of the kitchen. He made his way up to the workstation desk and let his eyes scan everything that was visible. He spotted a chart that was titled **Patient Meal Instructions.** He looked around and no one else was near so he put the silverware rack down and picked up the chart.

There were many names and room numbers on three typed pages, but he was only looking for one. Near the bottom of the second page he found a listing for, Jane Doe, Rm# 222.

Otis's heart skipped a beat. He had found her room!

He replaced the chart where he found it and moved away from the office area, looking for the serving carts. Twenty feet to his right, he saw a row of four-wheeled aluminum carts next to a hallway entrance leading out of the kitchen.

He then looked for and found the dish room where, stacked on a drying shelf were stacks of Cambro 12" ivory Cam-covers, the round fiberglass covers that are placed over a plate of food to keep the food warm and safe from contamination.

Otis grabbed a cover off of the shelf and then a clean plate from a rack of clean plates.

Placing the plate on the four wheeled cart and

covering it with the cam-cover, he wheeled the cart out of the kitchen and down the hall to find an elevator. So far, so good. He was beginning to feel very happy with his success..

The hallway he was in was quiet for this time of day. Coming around a corner Otis met a kitchen worker who was coming back from somewhere, pushing a large heated food cart. Otis pushed his smaller cart over to the right to let the larger cart pass with ease.

The employee, a twenty something man with a tattoo on his arm that said **BIG DOG,** saw Otis and stopped. "Hey dude, where's your name tag?" He was tapping his own tag with his hand. "That's a good way to get your ass chewed, I can tell you that!"

Otis reached up to his chest pocket where he would wear a name tag and put a surprised look on his face. "Oh no, I must have lost it! I had it on earlier, dammit!"

"Where you headed with just one plate?" the worker asked.

He was being a jerk, but Otis played along and acted like he was reading an order on his cart. "A special order for Room 222".

"Well, that ain't so far. I'd get that up there and back to the kitchen before Twirly catches you!"

Otis nearly fell back ward against the wall.

"Who did you say?"

"What the hell, you deaf? Twirly! The boss from corporate. He's here today. Twirly Jenkins."

Otis played dumb and replied, "Jeez, I must be getting old and forgetful. I remember now, thanks!"

Big Dog looked at Otis oddly and continued on his way back to the kitchen.

Otis stood there momentarily wondering if the boss Twirly was the same Twirly that had visited him so long ago and introduced him to time travel. Twirly had been instrumental in him meeting Sara during a time jump to Colorado. Could it be the Twirly he came back to help?

Because he had come back, he lost touch with Sara. They had lost touch until they were reunited as different species and now he was close to reversing that difference.

Surely this Twirly wasn't that one! He would investigate, but now he was looking for Sara. Otis found the freight elevator and took it two floors up. He wheeled the cart out onto the hallway floor and read a sign on the wall that told him rooms 215 -230 were to the right and 200 -214 were to his left. He went down the hall to the right and stopped outside room #222.

The door was partially closed so he knocked and pushed it open wide enough to enter with the aluminum cart. Otis was pleased to see that the first bed was not occupied. The woman in the bed next to the window had her bed raised to allow her sit up. She was sitting and quietly looking out the window. As Otis entered the room, she did not acknowledge his presence.

"Sara?" Asked Otis in a low voice.
She did not turn in his direction or reply.
"Sara is that you?" He was a little louder this time.
This time she turned to look at him, making Otis step backwards.
It wasn't Sara and it surprised him so, he nearly lost his balance.

"I'm sorry, I have the wrong room." He said politely and backed the cart out of the room. In the hallway he looked at the room number and sure enough it was number 222. Otis then noticed there was a paper tag attached to a clip next to the door. It had a name printed on it:

JANE DOE
#222
General Diet

Otis's mind reeled. They had given Sara the name Jane Doe. Who was this person? He pushed the cart down the hall and found a janitor's closet where he placed the cart and left it. He made his way to the ICU.

Still dressed as a kitchen worker, he was able to move about without causing any suspicion. He went down to the first floor and walked directly to the ICU. Peering into the unit, he could see that all four of the cubicles were empty, but as luck would have it a nurse sat in the nurse's station working at a computer.

Otis did not hesitate, he walked up to the counter. "Excuse me" he said. "Do you know what happened to the last patient that was in that bed?" He pointed to cubical #1 where Sara had been.

The nurse, a black woman in her fifties dressed in scrubs looked up at Otis and sighed. "I'm gonna have to check. I just came back from my weekend. It's Monday for me."

"Sorry." Otis replied. "I know what you mean."

"Oh don't be sorry, honey, it's all part of the job." She immediately tapped in a code on the computer keyboard and the information she was seeking came up on her screen.

"Let's see. Oh yeah, that was that young Jane Doe. Looks like she was a code black."

Otis's mouth dropped open. "She died!?"

"Mm hmm. No ID. Did you know who she

was?"

Otis shook his head and thanked the nurse as he left the ICU. He was in full shock and denial as he walked aimlessly down the hallway.

How could she have died? She had become human again. The Source had done as promised, but then why did she put herself in a position to be killed in an accident?

Tears flooded his eyes and he had to stop walking. He wanted to scream, but didn't. A cleaning department employee saw Otis leaning against the wall in distress and came up to him. "Hey man, you all right? Can I help you?"

Otis took a deep breath and wiped the tears from his eyes with the back of his shirt sleeve. "I'm okay, thanks. I just lost a good friend." Otis knew the excuse he was giving was the truth.

"I'm sorry for your loss." the cleaning employee said patting Otis on the shoulder before moving on down the hall way.

Otis was still wearing his kitchen uniform over his street clothes and made his way back to the kitchen. He wanted to leave, but he had to get a look at the Twirly person who was in charge before he left.

It was now closer to noon and the kitchen was as busy as it gets. Cooks and servers worked in unison putting together meal trays of steaming food that would be taken to the hospital cafeteria as well as the patient rooms.

Otis looked across the large room to the office and could see someone seated at the desk with his back to the doorway.

He made his way toward the office, going through a maze of work tables and serving carts, until he was just outside the door. The person sitting at the desk was on the telephone and Otis still couldn't see his face.

From the back, the small profile of a man sitting at the desk looked to be the right size of the man he met long ago, but it just can't be, Otis told himself again.

Otis looked around the small office for pictures or plaques that might give him a clue, but saw nothing. Then the man hung up the telephone, stood, and turned toward Otis.

Otis's mouth dropped open. It was Twirly, the Twirly he knew! "Twirly?"

The little man's eyes focused on Otis and then with a quivering lip, said, "Flagg!"

Twirly pulled Otis into his office and shut the door so no one could hear them talking.

Twirly was the first to talk. "Flagg, I can't believe it is you. You came back!"

"Yes. I'm back. I came back long ago when I was told you might be trapped in this time plane, but I couldn't find you and I left again."

"Otis. You are partially right. I'm trapped in this time plan, but it was of my own choosing. I decided not to return to my time plane."

"You chose to stay?" I don't understand." Otis was confused.

"It is a long story for another day. What's confusing is, what are you doing here," he looked at Otis's uniform. "What are you doing here in a hospital kitchen uniform?"

Otis rolled his eyes, "God, I don't know where to start. Have you got a few minutes?"

Twirly winked. "Time is what I got."

Otis started from the time he met Sara in Colorado and her plight as a feline after he'd returned to find Twirly. He continued through the time where he'd met the Source to arrange for Sara to regain her human self, right up to finding out Sara had just died.

Twirly sat and listened compassionately and when Otis finished he sat back in his chair and asked him, "Now what?"

Otis was at a loss for words and just shrugged and shook his head.

Twirly leaned forward and put a hand on Otis's shoulder. "You know my friend, all living beings die. Sadly some of us die young. Your friend Sara may have left here in death, but may still be living on a different plane. If you remember when we first met, you only

had three days left before you were going to die. Do you remember that?"
Otis shook his head yes.
Twirly continued. "You managed to defy that by traveling to a different plane, thereby altering the time here in this present.
And now that you've returned, your end of time will reset, if it hasn't already."
Otis put his head down. The way he was feeling at the moment that didn't sound so bad. "If that's the case, I'm ready."
"Are you now?" Twirly sat back and tilted his head. "Just gonna say fuck it! Is that it? Otis, you told me that when you visited The Source he had said that maybe you'd have something else to do, right?"
Otis nodded yes.
"Well then I would use my remaining time and go through the portal once more. Who knows what or who you might find. Living is all about discovery!"
Otis took a deep breath and let it out slowly.
"What about you?"
"What about me?"
"What have you discovered?"
Twirly got his devilish grin back. "A ha, I've discovered a life I love. You must do the same, my friend!"
The two sat in silence as Otis re-examined his priorities. Then Otis extended his hand in thanks.

"Thank you, for helping out an old man."
"Well you're not getting any younger sitting here, the best to you Otis!"
Otis stood up, removed the kitchen uniform and left the hospital. His time was short and he had places to go and places to see.

The Portal

Otis arrived home just after 5 pm and was able to enter his house without interference from Margie. As much as he disliked her constant mothering, he realized she did it for his own good. He realized if he should die, it would most likely be her and her husband Bill that would find his body if he was to shed it.
He had made all the proper arrangements for his remains and had unbeknownst to them, transferred his bank funds to them upon his death. He didn't like thinking about such things, but at 72, the "some day" he had always talked about had arrived.
In case he never returned, he made a final tour through the house, ending up in his study. In his desk drawer he had kept an envelope addressed to Margie and Bill that explained his wishes and gifts to them. He took it out and placed it on the desk top. Next he removed the blue bottle from its place in the desk drawer and took it into the living room.
He sat in his favorite easy chair and thought of

all the good times he had had in his life. The good had certainly outweighed the bad. Life had been good.

A knock on the door interrupted his thoughts.

"Otis, you in there?" It was Margie.

Otis quickly worked to remove the cork from the bottle.

Margie, I don't have time for you he was thinking as the cork finally released from the neck of the bottle.

Nothing happened! Otis tapped the bottle, and still nothing happened, it was just an empty bottle.

Margie was standing in the doorway. "The portal is gone, Otis."

Otis looked up in confusion, "I don't understand. How do you know what......."

Margie cut him off. "The time is right for me to explain." She came into the room and put her hand on Otis's shoulder. "Otis, you have known me as your next door neighbor, Margie. In truth I came into your life to watch over you. Margie is just one of the life forms I used. In reality I am the source Twirly told you about. I am your source."

Otis was dumbfounded. "Source? You?"

"Yes. As your source I was many things. I was the light you talked to asking for help for your friend. I was also the woman named Michelle you became infatuated with. And I too was the bounty hunter you killed. Only you didn't really kill me Otis, it just appeared that way in your eyes. For you, it was survival.

Otis became very somber as he tried absorbing all this information. Margie sat down on the chair closest to him.

Finally Otis spoke, "Why did you kill off Sara? For what reason would she need to die?"

"Otis all I can tell you is that here and now, it wasn't her time. She being here created a time warp of sorts and so her being was shifted to a previous time plane."

"So she still lives?" Otis's far away gaze shifted to Margie.

"Yes. She lives. We never truly die in the sense of non existence, we merely transcend to a different time."

Otis was now leaning forward in his chair. "I am so relieved to know she wasn't killed." His eyes brightened as he reached out for Margie. "Will I ever see her again?"

Margie smiled at Otis and for an instant Otis saw his mother smiling at him. She took his hand. "Yes Otis. Your time here has come to an end. The sun will be setting soon and I believe you have something of mine."

Otis wasn't sure what she meant at first then he remembered the green crystal frog in his desk drawer.

"Yes, yes I do! It is in my study, in the desk drawer! I nearly forgot about it."

"Okay good," Margie answered. "When the sun sets soon, you will use the portal in the green crystal frog to go back to a different time. You will find your friend Sara there."

Otis's eyes fought back tears.

In their remaining time together they discussed the letter Otis had written and about leaving them all his worldly goods. It was also planned how his "death" would be published in the local paper and a story would run about his life and times. There would also be a news story of his cremation, thus no one would ever come looking for his body. In the coming months Margie and Bill would sell and move away. No one would be the wiser of anything that had ever taken place.

As the sun began to set, Otis placed the green frog in the windowsill and turned to look at Margie.

"I don't know what to say." he said.

"You don't have to say anything. Time takes care of itself. You will soon forget me and this meeting. Time allows us to move on into the future and the future is where we belong."

The sun reached the exact point on the horizon and its rays began to hit the green crystal frog.

Seconds later a portal opened within the reflected light. Otis stepped into the light and quickly turned to wave at Margie, but she was already gone. An instant later all was black.

TOGETHER AGAIN

It was dark and cold. He was standing next to a small tree and only a short distance from where he stood he could hear the sounds of fast moving water. It all came back to him! He was standing by the pee tree, back in Colorado! He turned and could see the light of the campfire. Was he really back in this time or was he dreaming? Then he saw her. On the far side of the fire stood Sara, hands to her face. Was she crying?
"Sara, I'm here!" he called out.
She looked up and seeing him, rushed to his arms. "Otis! I thought you had left me!

They embraced and held each other. Otis was now positive he had entered the time plane he had left. The tears of happiness flooded his eyes.
PC and Katie saw them and joined them.
"O, you bastard, where did you go?" PC asked jubilantly. "We thought you'd been abducted by a flying saucer or something! Come on man, come back by the fire and warm up!"
Otis, with his arm around Sara smiled and

replied, "Throw another log on the fire we are on our way!"

He then took Sara and joined the others gathered around the campfire. The burning wood crackled and popped, sending sparks up into the night sky toward the millions of stars twinkling above them. He was finally with Sara and the future was before them.

Otis held Sara close to him and gazed at the stars above, knowing each one carried with it the promise of time!

ABOUT THE AUTHOR

Brian Peterson retired in 2010 from the general work force and lives in central Minnesota with his wife, Judy and their Dog Ben and Cat Kiwi. He likes good books, movies, pro sports, and traveling.

Questions or comments about Otis Flagg can be sent to: otisflagg@gmail.com

Otis Flagg and the Promise of Time

BRIAN PETERSON

Made in the USA
Monee, IL
13 May 2020